Acknowledgements

To all those who have been a part of my life: thank you from
the bottom of my cold dead emo heart. I wouldn't be the
same without you. You're all inspiration

The Hero of the Sword

By Chung Moon

.

Introduction

A long time ago, the accomplishments of one man and his tribe was the seed that would give birth to a mighty empire that spread across the known world, and it expanded across the stars.

It was a story that became legend. The tale of the Mighty Hunter was known to every person, in the most remote corners of the world. Though there is not much known about the origins of the Hunter; he and his twelve brothers grew their family into a tribe.

The Mighty Hunter was strong. During a time where demons ruled the lands, they did not dare get close to him. The rumors of his deeds reached the skies; God had a plan for the Hunter.

One night the Hunter received a call from the heavens to slay a demon that ruled its land with tyranny. The beast was immense. It measured two stories tall of demon--powered muscle. Its hide was virtually impenetrable, and the four horns emanating from its head were harder than any substance known, and the red glow that they emitted was said to be blood of other demons it ha d slain.

In order to defeat the beast, the Hunter and everyone in his tribe were gifted with powers beyond their potential. They were given the ability to use magic.

Even the Hunter was afraid of the creature. Its roar alone was intimidating, but the spirit of the Hunter was strong. And so, with hunger for fighting, the Hunter rode to the challenge. The Hunter's soldiers were wiped out in an instant, but at the end of the fight, their faith triumphed, and only the Hunter and few of his brothers were standing over the beast's corpse.

The Hunter and all of his people were then blessed with the powers of magic forever. He became a great king, he expanded his kingdom beyond the known horizon, and he lived in prosperity for many years.

Body

Chapter 1 -- *Colony Twenty Two*

Everything fell apart when I received a message:

'Hey, are you ok? There is a report that colony twenty--two is being attacked by demons. Is that where you are based? Please, write me back -- Gaya.'

Technological advancements increased exponentially thanks to the limitless potential that ethereal energy -- magic powers -- allowed. One of those advancements was telecommunication. The *telecom trinket* was a small device that allowed people across worlds to be able to send each other written messages, have voice conversations, or even see each other. Regardless of physical distances, communication was immediate. This trinket came in any form the person desired. I chose to wear mine as an ear piercing so I wouldn't lose it.

Gaya made fun of my choice when I first got it. She said something like "Wow, it suits you perfectly; it may even get you a boyfriend someday."

Gaya had a beauty of her own: small flat nose; big brown eyes; skin that changed tone dramatically depending on sunlight (and mood); and boobs that were hard not to stare at -- not too big, they just let their presence be known. But it wasn't the fact that she had lips that mine desired; it was her unique way of being that engraved her into my thoughts. She ate like an animal, with absolutely no etiquette. She laughed and joked as if no one was around. She was loud and obnoxious. I could spend hours with her and never get tired. She was a surprise in my life since I enjoyed being

4

alone. Even my best friends ended up draining me after what I would consider to be too many hours together.

Gaya had already rejected me a couple of times already. I feel it was my fault. I kept messing things up, and then time ran out.

I guess that was for the best, she was back on Earth. I was on colony twenty--two, far out in deep--space. We were both assigned to our respective posts by the Empire after our graduation at the Academy -- Gaya had graduated three years after I did. We didn't really have a choice. That is why we were all in that school; to train our abilities. Our line was descendent from the Hunter's tribe; the bloodline that could use magic. The only other way to be gifted with magic was being related to demons.

Gaya was well capable of utilizing the mystic arts, most of my friends were, but I on the other hand had barely made it through. Somehow I ended up as a high--ranked grunt on this space colony.

'Are you OK?! Answer me! -- Gaya'

I tried replying her that everything was fine, maybe a false alarm, but right at that moment I felt the ship shake in an unfamiliar, terrifying manner accompanied by an ear-- busting siren, a warning message, and red flashing lights. I froze for a second, trying to figure out what was going on or what to do. How could a ship this huge be in any form of danger, especially when we're so far away from any demon presence? I tried going back to Gaya's first message, but in that instance I received another message.

'Where are you? -- Shamain'

Oh, no. Her words brought me back to my senses. Shamain was a friend from back in the Academy. She had just arrived with the new batch of troops.

I had to make sure she was out of harm's way (though she was probably better off than me).

Though I hadn't really spent much time with her from the time since we had known each other, but somehow I got to care about her, and, well, I liked her a lot. I tried getting in contact with her, but she didn't answer.

I was on my floor, headed towards my room when the chaos started. Her room was in the rookie quarters, which was located in the lower floors. She was ten minutes away from me; that's if I took the elevators, but they were shut down, so I would have to hit reach the main lobby -- the central hub of the ship -- to reach the emergency passage way. I tried rushing, but it was difficult to get around the masses of people who were on a chaotic rampage to get to the lifesaver vessels. I tried reaching to her again over the telecom, no answer.

I could barely move towards the main lobby. People were jamming the corridors. All the lifesaver vessels were towards the south of the residential floors, the lobby was to the north. People were pushing each other. People were fighting, throwing things at each other. Those who fell got trampled on the floor; the screams of terror were getting to me. It was getting bloody. The problem with Shamain's floor was that the closest vessels for her were at my level. The design of the ship when it came to emergency situations was just horrible.

Panic started to take over me, and then I got slapped in the back of my head.

"Get it together! Now is not the time to panic." Umaso said. "Get your gear ready"

I joined Umaso and Sonja, we started heading towards the main lobby. There were other troops that got in with Umaso, but they stayed in order to help control the chaos.

"Where in the world were you?" said Sonja "we've been trying to contact you."

"What's going on?" I asked

"Demons have breached through the engine room. I don't know how, but that's not the problem right now" Sonja said. "I thought something happened to you, why didn't you respond to the radio?"

"I didn't receive anything, let me…"

"You can check that later" Umaso interrupted me. "Right now our mission is to intercept any hostiles from reaching our civilians."

Umaso and Sonja were the two closest friends I had met on this ship. Umaso was a prodigy soldier; he was the youngest candidate ever to be ever assigned to the Martial Horses -- the Empire's top--notch military division. He was actually younger than me, but he had already been in service for more than three years by the time he got in the ship. There was no distinction of rank between us -- except of course when he felt like using his rank to order me around. He had a strange sense of humor; he used to come out as rude more than anything.

We were about to reach the entrance to the lobby. I was feeling an intense need to find Shamain; this need was something I had never felt before; it was like I was hypnotized. I even forgot everything else that was happening. Without realizing it, I was running ahead of my teammates.

"Watch out, right in front of you!" I realized Umaso was at least twenty paces back.

At that moment I felt a fist molding my face, surprised I didn't lose my teeth. I got my ass knocked to the ground. A second of blindness when I opened my eyes, a demon-- zombie was looking down at me with its dead yellow eyes, covered in pus. I saw a face so full of murderous desire that its face was bleeding through every orifice, ready to gut me alive.

Demons had really gotten inside the bridge. See, the thing with demons is that they could or could not have a physical body; when they don't they take over other living beings -- humans were no exception. The more demons in a single subject, the stronger it gets, but the more damage it does to the body. The good news was that if the body is destroyed, any demons inside 'died'. The body in front of me had at least thirty demons inside. I had actually never seen a human zombie before that day./

My face was numb, it was already swelling. As the zombie started to rush attack me I reached for my hand cannon, I pulled the trigger, but it didn't shoot -- I forgot to load it. I then unsheathed my sword, but the zombie knocked it out of my hand. The zombie grabbed me by my vest; it opened its mouth, ready to take possession over me.

The zombie's hand was reaching for me. I flinched. Then I felt a gust of wind blow past me. It was Umaso's sword cutting the zombie's head clean. Umaso, my squad's captain, the lightning justice, certainly he had the blood of a hero.

He possessed a very unique ability. His incredible speed did not come from his legs. He could alter the physics in the matter that he could move towards any target he chose within his range in a blink. It was almost like teleportation, but he did have to physically move to the location.

Umaso was generally nice to those around him, and he would go the extra mile if someone needed help. He wouldn't have problems getting a girl either, but he didn't show any interest --which led me to guess about his sexual orientation. I mean, I had seen him in the showers. The bastard was ripped. Ripples of muscular texture adorned his body, even when he wasn't flexing. And since it's the showers… well, I'll just say he was well endowed in case

8

you wanted to know --some girls had asked me before; moving on.

Sonja was second in command in our squad. She was also an adept magic user, but her true genius was in her baking. Her red hair was a sign of her Northern origins -- like her people, she was tall and had a solid body. I liked to verbally abuse her, I was lucky she understood my sense of humor; otherwise I would have been turned into pulp a long time ago.

Umaso's rank could be compared to that of a captain. Sonja was a first lieutenant. One would wonder why she didn't have her own squad, but I knew why. She had a thing for Umaso, but he didn't budge.

Sonja rushed in front of Umaso, and then released her 'cookie shot,' a massive energy blast using her custom hand cannon -- Sonja's hand cannon was similar to my standard issue, but because of her superior output ability, she had to mod hers. Cookie was the name she gave to her own blast, girl stuff.

"How is the situation at the main hall?" Umaso called on the radio, but we could only hear noise from the response.

"This is bad; zombies shouldn't be near this wing." Umaso said. "Let's hurry"

"What's gotten into you?" Sonja yelled at me while she helped me get up.

I couldn't really explain it myself; I'm usually the guy who stays behind. We kept moving, when I had to say it "I… I have to get to the lower levels."

"The rookie quarters?" she asked aggravated. "Listen, no one's left there, they were all assigned to assist the civilians. Right now they should be on the escape vessels"

"You can't go there right now, we need to hold ground." Umaso paused "Fucking hell dude, we are undermanned, and now you want to go down there?! I risked the entire operation just to get your ass back!"

"We were worried you know!" Sonja added.

"That's exactly why! I'm worried" I snapped back.

He didn't respond.

Soon after, we reached the main lobby where the barricade was set. There were soldiers stationed across the area, waiting for an attack. Dead bodies, twisted from possession, were spread across the floor -- mainly from the north side where the technical areas were located. There was a violent friction in the air.

Umaso approached one of the officers.

"Sir!" the soldier greeted "We've managed to contain a wave of zombies, but there may be more heading this way."

"How in the hell did you let zombies get past you!" Umaso yelled; the officer was out of words. "Well it doesn't matter now." He continued "Shut the gates to the residences down, there doesn't seem to be anyone else."

"Yes sir!" and he left.

He turned to me "If you need to check on her, then you're gonna have to go by yourself."

"Thanks." I felt a relief.

"Make sure you contact back to us if you see anything."
Sonja said

"Try to make it quick; as soon as the civilians clear we will be heading towards the hangar." Umaso said "See you there."

Three soldiers assisted me to the residential gates, made sure the entrance was clear.

One soldier stopped me "Call us back so that we can open the gate back for you. Good luck."

"Thank you" and I headed in.

The intensity of my search wore down a bit.

There was an intense silence when I reached the rookie quarters. Only the emergency lights were on, so I could barely see. There was no one in sight when I looked around the corridors. I was moving as quietly and quickly as possible. Then I noticed a figure rocking back and forth in the fetal position, her face was covered.

"Hello?" I called out from the distance.

She didn't respond; I swallowed.

"Are you ok?" I asked again as I started getting closer; my hands could almost reach her shoulder, my cannon ready.

"NO!" she screeched out, and she swung her dagger at me.

"Stop, stop!" I yelled as I flinched back in fear. "I'm here to help you!"

Her facial expression showed desperation and fear. She had been bleeding from her forehead, and her eyes were blood-- shut from tears.

"Are you alone? Is there anyone else here?" I asked

"I... I don't know..." She started to speak very fast. I couldn't understand what she was saying, so I interrupted her.

"Calm down. Head upstairs to the main lobby. Once you're there use your trinket so they can open the gate for you."

"I don't have it with me... I don't know..." She started going off again.

"Hey, everything is going to be ok. Here…" I handed her my trinket. "Hurry up before move away from there."

She left quickly -- sheesh, not even a thank you -- as she left I resumed my search for Shamain. I realized how dumb of an idea that was. I could have just called Umaso to help get that girl. Now I had just lost my only way to get back with the squad. I could only keep moving forward -- the things that I do for a pretty face…

I reached Shamain's room. The door was closed. I knocked, but no answer. There was no light coming out from under the door. I stood in front of her entrance for what felt to be an eternity.

I figured that there was no one inside. I felt a bit of relieved; she was probably gone from the ship. But I decided to be completely sure.

I busted the door with my cannon. Before I snuck my head to check, I heard a voice.

"That's no way to get inside a lady's room."

It was Shamain.

Chapter 2 -- *Shamain*

 She was sitting on her bed. The light on her room was off.
I could only see her silhouette. Her eyes had a faint white
glow that I had never seen. I felt a chill in my back. Those
eyes had an eerie feel about them.

I was afraid of the worst. I raised my weapon as a
precaution, not sure that I could have shot even if I had to.

"Are you gonna shoot me?" she said, not amused.

I turned on the light, hoping she had not been taken over by
demons.

Her eyes were back in their silver color. Her skin, white as
milk, was flawless. Her golden hair flowed from her head
like waves of silk down to her back. Her slim fragile figure,
seeming delicate, gave away impalpable strength. She was
beauty that should be forbidden.

I lowered my cannon.

"No, sorry... I was afraid you had been turned into a
zombie..." I started to sweat a little, seeing her so radiant
was making me nervous. My voice was starting to stumble,
trying to hide my relief and joy. "How come..."

"I'm ok" she said softly as she was slowly getting up. "I
wanted to see you here, all for myself."

Her words were melting my insides. I forgot to consider the
strangeness of the situation as she was slowly approaching
towards me, seductively. I didn't even question what she
was still doing in her room in such an emergency. I had
forgotten all about it. Instead I asked.

"Since when do your eyes glow white?"

"Do you like them?" She placed her hands behind the back of my neck.

"I guess…" I started wondering why she was buttering me up-- not that she needed to -- but I wasn't against it either.

Her face was now very close to mine.

"It happens when I have my prey in sight."

In an impulsive, almost involuntary thought, I did what I had wanted to for so long. I kissed her.

Her lips started moving with mine; I could feel her moisture like sweet nectar. My heart started beating like I had just run a marathon. My limbs were weakening. I was in my own little heaven. A moment I could only dream of; I wanted that moment to last forever.

I dropped my weapons, and held her body tightly. It was more like I was holding on to her so I wouldn't fall. I could feel her breath on my skin, soothing my swollen face. I had never felt anything softer than her lips. I never knew a kiss could feel this way.

My head was spinning in pure delight. I felt my heart get closer to hers.

"Not bad" she said, and we kissed again.

Her lips were suddenly cold and hard. I was feeling strangely weak. Her mouth was starting to feel dry, and it was as if it was sucking the moisture out of my face. It was then when I realized my life force was being drained. The sting was numbingly painful. I tried pulling back, but I couldn't. I lost the feel on my limbs, and her grip was tightening. I was starting to asphyxiate.

I was lights out for a brief moment. Next thing I knew, I was laying on the floor, face down. I could barely move. My entire body felt numb except for a burning pain in my left arm. I had difficulty breathing from the position I was in. I moved so my face was on my side. I noticed my hand--cannon near my reach.

I saw Shamain standing in front of me, her back towards me. She moved her hair to the side; showing her *BES* unit embedded below the back of her neck, right above her shoulder blades.

A *BES* or "bodily entry storage" unit is a magic--based device about the size of the palm of a hand. It allowed the magic user to store items inside his/her body. Think of magic backpack. The bigger the user's magic output granted a larger storage capacity. It was a rather complicated device, and the concept behind it terrified me. I feel sorry for the first experiment subject who was assigned to use one.

She pulled out a sword -- I had seen that sword before -- The sword was rusted, and it didn't seem to be able to cut anything. It was almost the length of her body; the fuller of the blade was as wide as her torso, and it didn't seem to have a guard. Somehow she didn't have any problems wielding it.

Soon after, a dim white light started to cover the sword, and in almost an instant -- as if the layers of rust peeled away -- the sword regained its vitality. It was a vibrant sword, shining with its own light. I could feel its power, the sharpness of the blade made it seem like it was vibrating, and it hurt my eyes.

"Beautiful, isn't it?" she said.

"Yes, you are."

In that instance, I grabbed my cannon with my left hand, and aimed at her. My grip was shaking.

"Are you gonna shoot me now?" She didn't even move. "You really should."

I dropped my arm.

"You know I can't." My voice was shaking. "J... Just what is going on?"

I thought she would finish me then, but instead she turned around, shut off the lights, and she turned her face to me for a brief moment. Her eyes were brighter than before. I managed to gather enough strength to call her between breaths before she left.

"What would you do to attain the power to awaken, control a god; the power to change a dying world? Someone like you, who doesn't even know; someone who can't even see past himself does not deserve to have that power." She said it frighteningly calm.

"I... I don't..."

"Whatever, I don't have the time for this, I got other shit to do."

"Shamain..."

She waited for me to say something, but I didn't know what. I didn't know what she was talking about. Her eyes had a cold stare in them. I couldn't recognize them. I couldn't reach them. I didn't say anything.

She turned around and left.

The irony, I had imagined many times to have Shamain's room to be my last resting place, but the original idea was to have her by my side. I just laid there motionless.

Chapter 3 -- *Flashback: the incident at the Barren Lands*

I forgot to introduce myself. My name is Hadassah, but
people called me Jack, or Jackie. I couldn't remember why I
got the new name. It's much easier to pronounce, so I didn't
mind. At least I didn't go by Cheese, someone else did. It's
a little strange to be describing myself, but just in case you
want to know. I was rather short back in the Academy days;
back then Alon was taller than me, but once I hit space - not
sure if the gravity had anything to do with it - but I grew
taller. I wasn't the most handsome walking on two feet, but
I wouldn't say I could be considered ugly; like, people could
look at me without making a weird face. I always had a
horrible hair do. No matter how much I tried to style it - I
used *demon wax*, potent stuff -, the back of my hair would
go back to its original style. But my biggest personal issue
was my body; it was well on the underdeveloped side - that
never changed no matter what. A small package didn't
inspire too much confidence either. It was not until that
encounter with Shamain where I didn't know I had some
hidden ability within me. I couldn't figure out what she was
talking about or what did I have to do with changing the
world, or some ancient sword. It was then when it hit me.

As I lay on the floor lost in thoughts, I remembered the day
that I saw Shamain's sword for the first time. It was back in
the days of the *Academy*.

Physical proficiency exams were about to start soon. These
exams were to test the individual's ability with *magic*; and to
be qualified as an *ethereal user* -- someone with a
substantial ability to use *magic* -- there was a certain degree
of proficiency that I barely passed. Without this
qualification, I wouldn't have been able to *be* someone. To
make things worse, the head of the disciplinary committee
was the one running the exams. That hard--ass was so strict
I was afraid he would not let me pass.

The exams were rigorous, so it was highly recommended to gather up some magic prior. *Ethereal energy* was the source of all our magic powers and technology. An *ethereal user* could gather and store this energy from the surrounding environment.

I had problems concentrating inside the Academy's facilities, so for the past days I had been training outside the city, in the barren lands of the *Last Stance of the Rebels*. Three thousand moons ago, this barren land was the place where the last major offensive of the resistance against the empire took place. The battle was fought hard, and thousand died there; but it was said that the fighting spirit of those warriors still remained.

I was told it was a good place to train since the air here was heavy on *ethereal energy*. I wondered how big of a battle it was; there was so much destructive magic force lying in the land that even after so many years barely any vegetation could grow. I was surprised that no one else had come here to train, but I didn't mind. I liked the quietness that the place brought. It helped me to not think about the uncertainty of my future or about my failure with Liora -- my old crush from my days at the Academy -- but for some reason, I couldn't stop thinking about Shamain. Though I knew her less then; I had already started caring about her.

For the moment, at least, I was just enjoying the peaceful feeling and not having to think much.

"Why do you hate me so much? Tell me!" I was so focused in my training that I hadn't noticed Gaya. Her face was full of anger, but it didn't face me.

Gaya was not a person who ever came into my mind, so I took a pause to identify her. You could say that I was a complete asshole towards her.

"Hate you? Isn't that too strong of a word to use? I don't even dislike you, but why do you ask me?"

"So then, why do you treat me so bad? And..." She stopped talking, and she turned away from me in embarrassment. Her face was red like a tomato. "Why are you naked?"

I was so unprepared to see anyone around here that I completely forgot I was naked. I mean, it was so warm and comfortable, but now it had all turned into an embarrassing moment.

"Shit! Give me a second" Now I had to explain myself "See, I thought it'd be easier to train if I exposed myself entirely to better intake the magic energy around me."

"Ok, but did you have to be butt naked? Gross!"

"What you mean gross? It's not like I thought anyone would be here!" I did enjoy being naked though. "Ok, you can turn around now. Wait, I forgot to put my underwear back. Turn around again"

She started laughing really hard. It felt strange. I was embarrassed, I had never been naked in front of a girl, but seeing her laugh with her shoulders shaking as if they were about to fall off. I found that to be cute while feeling insecure at the same time.

After the commotion, we sat down for a little bit, staring into the horizon, everything was quiet for a moment. I felt a strange peace take over me.

We stood there watching the sun set over the horizon.

She started laughing again "I can't believe you were naked."

"Hey, no one invited you here, so it's not my fault."

"It's ok. It's not like you're very exciting to look at." Ouch...

"So, do you hate me because of Alon?" She changed the topic.

Alon was one my closest friends whom I had grown up with. Gaya and Alon dated for a brief moment, but it then ended badly. I never found out the details as to what happened between them.

"No, damn it, stop using that word. Just think, I've been mistreating you long before Alon."

She paused. "Oh, I see."

"No, I just like to brush you off for fun. I never thought you'd take it so personally."

"Of course I have! All I've tried to do all this time is be nice to you, and instead you act as if you hate me."

"Why would you want to befriend me?" I said.

"I don't know. I just felt like we would get along."

That shut me up. I didn't have a smart--ass comeback for such sincere words.

She continued "so, you like to get naked to get a better feel on nature, huh. You're such a pervert. Does it feel good?"

"Hey! Seriously, what are you doing here? And yes, it feels great."

"I come around here sometimes. I felt your presence nearby, so I decided to come over." She was sensitive to other people's presence. I was one of her many skills. Gaya was a *magic* prodigy as well.

"So, I heard that you like Liora a lot, but now she has a boyfriend now. I'm sorry…" She said

"Yeah, it's ok though. She looks happy with him."

"Sorry, but am sure you'll find the right one someday. So, were you like in love with her?"

"I don't know; maybe, maybe no." I paused "Have you ever been in love?"

She paused for a moment "Yes, a long time ago. He was the greatest and coolest guy I ever met. I loved him."

"And, what happened to him?"

"Well, thing is… he was so talented. I heard people say that he was some prodigy, the type of talent that shows only once in a generation. I didn't care about that though." Her voice started to sadden. "The empire decided to take him away to some elite place. We tried running away, but to no avail. He promised to keep in touch, but I haven't heard from him since."

"Sorry. I don't know what to say… and I'm here sulking about some dumb crush."

"Wanna hear a secret?" she continued "I came to this Academy thinking that I could find him here… well, at least it was far away from the things that reminded me of him"

"Do you think of him a lot?"

"Yeah, every day… At least I like to think he is doing great; maybe he found someone else already." She smiled "Funny, I never really talk about him."

"Then thanks for sharing your story with me. And screw that guy. He is a dumbass for leaving you."

She laughed again. "Thanks. it feels alright talking to you."

"It's nice talking to you, too." I got curious "What happened between you and Alon though?"

"Don't tell anyone about this ok?" She got alert all of a sudden "Jack, get your gear ready."

I was perplexed at her reaction. "Why?" I asked.

"Just do it. We are in big trouble." She said as she pulled her weapons out from her *BES*. Hers was on her lower back.

She pulled out her dual swords, one of them she received as a gift from her lost love.

I couldn't spot the threat that got her so tensed up, but I could feel its presence looming on us. It was a very strong demonic aura. I tried to stand up, but I plummeted into the ground. I had never felt such pressure, such destructive power; all aimed towards me.

"Jack! Wake up!" she shielded me with her energy.

"Gaya, what is going on?" I asked.

"I don't know, but this is bad. This aura is way too strong. I don't know how long we can hold for" Her voice was shaking.

"This is not possible; no demon has appeared near Atlas City in years." My voice was trembling more than Gaya's.

A deep purple fog had covered the area. It was so thick that I could not see past ten paces. It felt like we entered a different dimension.

The fog was irritating on the skin. My legs fell like they were stuck in thick mud; I was breathing heavily, and I was losing strength. Gaya was standing next to me with both her swords unsheathed and stabbed on the ground, ready. She had her rifle--cannon aimed at the figure -- she used a long--barreled rifle, quite powerful, and suiting to her high energy levels. Her face was still and focused for battle, but her hands were clearly shaking.

"Gaya, we should get away from here…"

"No, we'll die if we try to run now. I've already called for help." She showed me her *emergency beacon* "But, why is this thing after you?"

I could hear that something was coming our way. It sounded like a piece of metal being dragged on the floor. The echo caused by the fog made the sound feel all the more terrifying. Each footstep approaching us invaded my ears.

A silhouette of a human appeared through the purple mist. It was of a big, muscular build. Bigger than any other person I had ever seen. The fog gave way to figure in front of us. Though it looked human, it felt more like a demon than anything. I then noticed that what this person was carrying was a huge, rusted sword.

The demon stopped in front of us; he was barely visible.

"Hello?" It was the only thing I could think of saying. Confused, the figure I was seeing in front of me did not seem real. The figure was dark; it looked more like a solid shadow than a body.

The demon replied with a vertical swing of the sword. Gaya pushed me away to the side. She barely dodged. We were displaced to the sides of whatever it was that was attacking us.

The figure stayed still for a moment after its first attack.

"I got it. Jack, this is not a demon. This thing is an ancient spirit; a wraith. But why... and that sword..."

Demon, ancient spirit, or wraith, it didn't matter. The spirit swung the sword at my head. It was fast. I froze there like an idiot. On that second Gaya blasted charge at the spirit's arm with her cannon.

The wraith turned towards Gaya, and it unleashed a flurry of swings. Gaya was able to keep up --she was surprisingly fast -- but the demon started to speed up and it gained ground. Eventually she got knocked to the ground. The spirit swung once more to finish her. I had to do something.

I didn't think about it. I drew my sword and I impaled it to the wraith into its back with every inch of strength and magic I could gather. It worked. It stopped the wraith in mid swing. The spirit then screamed a shrieking howl.

The wraith bitch--slapped me so hard I rolled on the floor. My sword was still stuck in its back, so I took that opportunity to cast an energy blast through my sword -- my friend, Sela, taught it to me.

The wraith was shrieking in pain, trying to pull my sword out. Gaya used this time to charge her cannon to the max. At that close range, she blew the wraith to pieces.

"Good job, Jack. You're much more talented than you look" she said a bit more mangled. "But, I don't know how much longer we can hold."

"What do you mean? Didn't you blow it up to pieces just now?"

"No, this is a wraith, and wraiths don't die, duh." She said it breathing heavily "The only way is to seal it away, but I don't have that ability… I don't know what to do."

The side of my face had gone numb. With Gaya's decreased strength; I could feel the pressure gaining on us. I was having trouble wielding my sword.

We weren't getting a moment to catch our breath. Gaya looked tired. She had already used up a lot of energy while using her rifle cannon, and protecting me from the aura must have taken a toll on her stamina. That sword… it was vibrating franticly. The wraith was taking back its shape. Suddenly, the figure in front of stopped moving. It just stood there.

"Jack, we won't make it at this rate. We need to get back to the city. We could use my umbrella to help us launch fast out of here, but I don't know which way the city is."

She was referring to her magic umbrella -- her personal travel method. When charged, the umbrella dispersed the air with enough power to carry heavy loads… another marvel

24

from magic. Though most people held on to the handle to float around; larger models allowed for you to sit on the canopy. It was a popular item among girls, but rather expensive.

"Why didn't you think of that before?" I asked

"It skipped me…" she returned a dumb smile at me

"I know which way is the city." I said. I had been coming to this same spot for a while now. "You see this rock? This side faces toward the city. But… the wraith is on the way."

"Do you trust me?" She smiled.

Gaya took out her umbrella and aimed it at the wraith with the canopy still closed. She then guided my hands to hang on to the handle. My hands were holding onto hers at the same time.

"Ok, then, hang on tight." We charged our energy, and we blasted forward.

At that second, the wraith swung its sword upwards. It didn't give us the time to react. It broke the umbrella. The force sent both of us flying in the air. Lucky the sword was rusty, we could have been sliced.

We landed like a sack of potatoes. Gaya took most of the impact, and she fell unconscious. I was still awake, but without Gaya's protection, the pressure was gaining on me. My thoughts were being consumed to a state where I was losing my own self.

The wraith was walking towards me, the sword dragging by its left. I felt that another entity was getting inside my head. The wraith in front of me was trying to communicate with me. For a moment, I could see past the shadows that veiled the person inside.

He was a warrior of times past. He was just as immense as his shrouded figure. Despite of his decayed state; there was

25

something noble about him. This ancient spirit seemed to be reaching for me, desperately.

The wraith's hand was about to grasp me, but it stopped. The figure started to dematerialize. Its body started to become translucent. I saw someone else standing behind the wraith. It was Shamain. The approached the vanishing warrior slowly until she was holding on to the wraith from behind, and just like that, the spirit vanished, and the fog was gone in an instant.

The only thing that remained was the sword, which looked nothing more than a rusty clad of iron.

She then approached me.

"You can rest now." She said it in a soothing tone "Help is on its way."

As soon as I heard her voice, my eyes started to close. The last I saw of her was that she checked on Gaya's vitals; she then picked up the sword, and then she left.

By the time I regained consciousness the sun had almost gone down completely.

"Hey Jack!" Gaya was sitting next to me. She was a little bruised, but she was smiling.

"You're finally up." That was Mr. Ham; a teacher at the academy, also known as the Legend from the East. "I came here as soon as I got Gaya's emergency call."

"What happened?" I asked.

"You got attacked by one of the ancient spirits that roam these lands. It's not safe to come around this area when there is a total lunar eclipse. Haven't you heard the warnings?" I was feeling a bit dumb.

"You're lucky that you survived the incident this time. Judging by Gaya's current shape; the spirit you faced was quite powerful. I wonder how you made it through." Mr. Ham said it in a reproaching tone.

"Where…" I stopped. For some reason I did not want to mention Shamain. I wasn't even sure if the person who saved us was her. It didn't make sense.

"Well, at least I am glad that you two are ok. Jack, Gaya told me about what happened. You kept your composure during this type of battle. I am quite impressed at both of your skills." He patted me on the shoulder. "Anyways, you should start heading back before it gets dark. I would go with you, but I have to go elsewhere, but here, I brought an extra umbrella just in case."

"Ok then teach, thank you so much for helping us." Gaya said in her usual radiant tone. She hugged him.

"Alright then kids. I'll see you in school" He waved, and left. I was still surprised he had come to our aid.

"Hey Gaya, so, do you have a crush on the teacher?"

"Oh my God" she said it in a flustered tone. "You're so stupid! I am going home by myself, bye!"

She took out a second umbrella, and she left.

"Hey, I was just kidding. Gaya! Wait! I'm scared!" I started running after her.

Strange, since when did she get the right to call me stupid? Before that day I had never thought I would find myself chasing Gaya.

How stupid of me. I just realized how idiotic the idea of giving up my trinket was. Now I was stuck in the rookie quarters, and I could see erratic movements belonging to demon zombies approaching. But I couldn't care. The incident with Shamain really shocked me; I never thought she would do that to me. I learned that day that real heart breaks can really devastate one's foundation.

I heard several explosions, each one getting louder than the next. Then saw body parts flying around outside the door. Smoke and debris covered my view. When the view cleared,a space vessel appeared in front of me. I thought I was hallucinating now. The only way it could have fit was by blowing up the entire area -- and that is exactly what Sonja described what had happened. Umaso came in to save my ass, again.

"Hmm... strange, I had never seen this kind of situation. Your left arm has gone completely useless. From the outside it looks like it's infected with necrosis, but it's still alive on the inside." Sonja said after running a medical diagnostic on me. "I still don't understand how this happened."

Funny, I had never told them that I had met Shamain, or what really happened. For some reason I had a tendency to avoid mentioning her to others; not on purpose, it just happened. They didn't ask either. They must have assumed I got attacked or something.

"Oh well... I guess I can't move my arm any longer" I didn't know what was going on with me. Losing complete use of one of my appendixes didn't even bother me one bit. I just couldn't get over feeling betrayed by someone I held so dear to me.

"Hey, cheer up. Too bad I don't get to chop one of your limbs off." She always tried to cheer me up, the bitch.

"Sometimes I don't know what kind of ideas go inside your head. Here, take this." Umaso handed my trinket back.

"Oh, thanks. Where is she?" I asked

"She is in another ship with other survivors. It's only us three in this ship, because we had to detour for your ass, again. Anyways, she sends her gratitude." He replied. "If we use the *portals* we should reach back home in a week."

Portals were huge rings that bent matter in the aid of transportation and communications. They were installed by the space colony throughout its route. I have fond memories of near death experiences when I was assigned to install those things.

"What about the ship?" I remembered I never saw Shamain make it out, and I never told the full story.

"Why, you're worried? You can see the ship crashing against that planet. I guess in the end, the ship hit its target." Umaso replied with his strange humor. "I don't understand why you're still thinking about that 'friend' of yours. But if you want my opinion, I'm sure she made it out fine."

I gave a sigh of relief, hoping to believe his words.

"Just rest up for now…" Umaso said. "Oh, you should try and meet with that girl you saved, she seemed quite interested in you, hero."

I should have had listened to that idea. Idiotic me forgot to contact her soon after. No, instead I decided to chase the impossible -- very smart…

I replied Gaya. I wanted to tell her about my last encounter with Shamain, but I was afraid that her reply would be the same as the others -- "forget about her" -- so after she told me to meet, I cut our conversations short. In the meantime I stayed laid in bed for two days. I was feeling very low. I even forced myself to sleep when I was awake; I was hoping that with time I would hear from Shamain since she wasn't replying.

"We are receiving transmission from a nearby ship. We have it on sight" Sonja said "Strange though, the empire hasn't dispatched any ships to this area."

'Is the 87th team on board? I'm looking for (corporal) Hadassah, is he there with you?'

The sound was a little choppy, but there was no mistaking it. That voice was Alon.

Alon was one of my two closest friends from back in my younger days and in the Academy as well. Along with Sela, the three of us grew up together, and they had seen me through thick and thin. Alon had a way with words. He was a rather charming individual, but had a commanding call that was at obnoxious and bossy. He would strike as a very intimidating man to those who didn't know him, and he had a very short temperament to boot. He was a bit chubby, and his face and eyes would get red when he got angry. I nicknamed him the *red bell pepper* -- he kicked my ass for it, and then he kicked my ass again when the name stuck, and once more just for fun.

"RBP (red bell pepper)!!" I yelled in excitement through the radio. "What are you doing out in space? Did you get placed around here?"

'No you dumb shit, I heard about your ship from Gaya. Dude, I tried leaving sooner, but I couldn't get a ship free... the space front is on a massive turmoil.'

"Opened a video communications channel" Sonja said

Do you know if any other ships have been attacked? How are colonies one through twenty one? Have they been attacked?" Umaso called on the radio.

'It's all bad news everywhere. Almost every ship has reported attacks, especially larger vessels. But they were minor compared to your case...'

"So wait, you spoke to Gaya?" I interrupted.

'Not really'

"This is bad. If the cause for all this is…" Umaso paused, and then turned to Sonja and I, "Do you remember the time I told you about the history files I found inside of the Martial Horses Central? I found information stating that the origin of our *ethereal energy* is not derived from the heavens, but it is much more similar to demonic powers instead."

"So, are you saying that demons have learned how to use *inception ores*?" I asked.

"Not necessarily, there is no evidence that they've ever had that ability; moreover, *inception ores* and *ethereal energy* itself have a 'repellent' or rather an incompatible nature for it to be any use for demons." Umaso said.

He had me lost there. *Inception ores* were the raw material that built civilization as we knew it. These ores made it possible for users to channel their own energy into an object, thus creating the action desired. The *inception ores* were processed, and refined into different materials that would be imbedded all sorts of objects such as *trinkets, BES* units, weapons, and even space ships. Almost every person in the empire was essentially able to use *magic* with the ability to make use of *telecom trinkets,* and other low--level tools such as lighting appliances. But only those that were gifted were able to channel *ethereal* energy in its more raw form in order to use more advanced tools such as *BES* units, or having the ability to manipulate *magic* in order to use advanced weapon abilities.

Some people like Umaso, were able to channel *ethereal energy* in alternate ways without the aid of these ores to a limited degree; his unparalleled speed is an example.

31

"When I kept researching on *inception ores,* I found out that in order to properly process an *inception ore* it requires the use of sealed demons." Umaso continued "what is really puzzling is the research that was done on these ores, and it showed that recently manufactured inception ores degrade much more rapidly than before."

"Those are some strong accusations… how could have this been passed by just like that?" Sonja added.

"The weakening never showed to be too drastic on small applications" Umaso said "but seems that the larger the concentration and capacity demanded on the ores causes an exponential chance of fail."

"Wait, wait, what are you guys talking about?" I asked

'What he means is that demons are starting to leak from these ores, you knob!' Alon shouted.

"Oh"

'It sounds like we should get out of orbit as soon as possible. Dock into my ship. This baby is much faster than that tiny little space coffin you're in.'

"Will do" Sonja replied "Let's get out of here"

'Right on, just give me a minute while I set up for boarding. It's only me on this ship right now…'

Alon left the ship's bridge. All we could hear were a bunch of noises… accompanied by a loud shriek belonging to his shower singing, then he stopped.

We heard shots, grunts, and things being violently thrown around.

'Argh… Die you mother fuckers!' then we lost connection.

"What the hell is this?" I cried.

A few moments of quietness, then the visual showed Alon's space ship blow up, and then more silence.

"I'm sorry" I felt Umaso's hand on my shoulder.

Before the feeling of loss started to sink in, the radio started buzzing again.

'Umm... I'm gonna need your help here' Alon shouted through the radio channel

Sonja zoomed in to where Alon's ship exploded, and there he was, piloting his custom *Leatonian War Suit* -- a compact *mech*a designed for close combat on anti--demon operations; it was about five times the size of an average person; and designed for use in outer orbit. Alon was frantically charging and swinging at *spirit demons*. There were at least twenty of them. *Leatonian* was a processed inception ore used in mechas and other vehicles.

The term *spirit demon* referred to a demon's original form. They were visible to the naked eye, but they didn't have a real body. They were considerably weaker than ones that had taken possession of a body, but they were harder to aim and take down; especially since they were invisible moments before they made an attack. In large numbers they were a big threat to anybody.

"Sonja, get a close to that *LWS* unit. Tow him in when I give you the signal. I'm going to assist." Umaso spoke quick and sharp. "Jack, get on the *LCU*; you're coming with me."

Not a word from me; I just followed the orders. A *LCU,* short for *Leatonian Civilian Unit,* was another *mecha* vehicle -- bulkier, slower than and twice as large as a LWS -- built for more civilian tasks such as construction, maintenance, and industrial. Umaso had taken one as a souvenir to help pick me up from the rookie quarters.

There was no need from assistance from Umaso and mine. When we reached to Alon, he had already felled most of the traceable hostiles, Umaso helped take down the rest before I caught up -- couldn't really pilot the LCU well without the use of my left arm. We hurried back to Sonja and left the site.

"I had to blow up the ship. There were just too many of those demons around" Alon said casually, still in his suit.

I glared at him for a second, stunned by his train of thought and current presentation.

"How did u manage to put on that suit so quickly?" He looked extremely crammed inside the core/cockpit of his suit, like he was canned inside.

Before he answered me; the core opened up, the suit's limbs compacted into itself and sooner than I could say "What the hell…" The entire LWS shrunk and vanished into Alon's BES unit, placed in his large round stomach.

"I didn't" he responded, clearly feeling sleek about his contraption. It was impressive.

Alon then accommodated in the ship, and got himself acquainted with the other two crew members. I had never been good at reading other people, and their intentions, but I swear that since that day Alon started to look at Sonja a little funny; not sure why.

Chapter 5 -- *Back Home*

I had dreamed of going back to the place where I grew up; visiting all my favorite places; seeing my old friends; seeing Gaya after so many years. Instead, we got questioned for suspicious activity once we arrived at the docks.

We got detained for a couple of days until they cleared our case. But lucky for us, Umaso was a Martial Horse, so we didn't get put into a quarantine section. He even helped clear Alon from losing his job; or ending up in death row from stealing and blowing up an imperial ship.

But once we got out, I wasn't too happy. I had wondered where Sela had been the past months since I hadn't heard from him. During detention Alon told me about his recent whereabouts, and it made me feel uneasy.

This is the last message that Sela had sent:

I can feel my demon blood boiling at nights. This cursed arm is starting to take over me. I can't control it anymore. I had to cut it off. Last night, a fourth arm spawned. This one had tissue missing, and the touch of air fills me in raging pain. I feel like I am transforming into something else.

My thoughts are being invaded by voices, hungry. But there is one voice, the voice of a woman, it is soft. It keeps telling me to go to the land of my ancestors. I need to go there, to the southern regions. This is the first time an adventure scares me. See you soon.

Sela had been many things, but I could never portray him being afraid of anything other than commitment. I couldn't blame him with so many choices flocking to him. Well, at least that's how it was last time I saw him.

I would guess that Sela was the more impressive between him and Alon. Sela was taller and more massive than Alon. Maybe girls were attracted his naturally bronze skin, or

35

maybe his dark red hair. That hair always made him look like a primal warrior who had just finished bathing in the blood of his prey. Then you add the muscles, a couple of punch--lines, and we have hundreds of love letters on his mailbox; and plenty of foot massages with oil.

Though Sela was one of my best friends, it took me a while to get over the fact that he was a half--breed. He had demon blood coursing through his veins. He was a direct descendant of the *Priestess of Light,* or so he said. It did take me a while to get used to that third arm of his -- the sign of his violent ancestry.

Half--breeds were considered to be inferior. He told me how tough his early childhood days were. I could only imagine; that birthmark of his was a tool that was used to be picked on by kids and adults alike. He got into countless of fights, but he stood strong against adversity, and he was proud of his inheritance. I would, too, if I was him. Apart from a superior ability to use magic, he could also use his demon powers. He could generate and extend countless of arms to come out of his body. He could use them with incredible dexterity, and then retract them when he was done. I don't think he'd ever used his powers to its full capacity.

No, there was nothing inferior about Sela. Up until the point I met Umaso, I never thought there could be anyone that could reach his level, but that's beside the point. He preferred to use his extra arm for other purposes. From observation, he was mostly comfortable cradling his hand on a girl's rear pocket.

I envied his ease with girls more than I did his strength.

I stood on the middle of the courtyard outside the space port's restraining facilities. The sky was clear and the sun was blinding bright. I was stupefied by a false sense of hope and peace the sight gave me.

"What are you gonna do?" Alon, he was always to the point.

I didn't know what to tell him. My first thought was telling him I was going to search for Shamain and find out the mystery behind her, but I wouldn't even know where to start. Or maybe I could go get my arm checked, but medical services were on chaos due to the recent space attacks. But what Alon really wanted to hear, and what my sense of duty was telling me, was to go look for Sela. I wanted to see Gaya, but in all, I was still part of Umaso's squad, so it wasn't my call.

"Maybe you should calm down, take some time to organize." Umaso said as he approached us. Sonja was behind him.

I could see Alon wasn't happy with that option.

"Listen," Umaso continued "I'm guessing you're going back to your work, steal another ship and head south. Sorry, I couldn't help overhearing your conversation."

"You think you know me?!" Alon's fist tensed. "Stay away from my own business!"

"Say you steal a ship, and then what. You'll probably end up dead before you find your friend, not that I think you could. And I wouldn't try stealing a ship. You'll be put to death for certain. This time I won't help." Umaso said "It was your friend's choice to be there."

Alon's face started to boil. He took a step toward Umaso, but then stopped. "No one's asked for your help, so go fuck yourself. Jack, what are you gonna do?"

I was quiet for a moment. "He's right Alon. We don't know where we went... I'd go, but..."

"I see," Alon started to walk away.

"I know someone who can help." I said "She can probably help us get a ride."

I knew Alon didn't like the idea, but he ceded and left.

Umaso turned to me. "You are under my orders; what gave you the idea that you can do whatever you please?"

I was frozen. I couldn't look him in the eyes. I was searching for a correct answer.

"I'm just kidding you dumbass!" Umaso laughed "Our squad's been dismissed the second we landed; no colony, no mission."

"Not funny…" I said

"You really put me in situations I don't want to be in. But I just can't let you go by yourselves, you'll get killed." Umaso scratched his forehead. "It will take two days to get authorization to leave."

"Ok, I'll let Alon know." I replied.

"Don't worry. I'll go tell him myself" Sonja quickly interrupted. "I have some things to do… and he's on my route."

She left in a hurry. I was confused by her strange generosity.

"Hmm, it's just as I suspected. She doesn't normally talk like that either…" Umaso said softly.

"You mean… them two?"

"Yes. Well, let's go get some food." Umaso said "By the way, who is this person you mentioned?"

Chapter 6 -- *Umaso/Aiyoo*

It was bittersweet being back on my home planet. It was nice revisiting all the places I used to frequent, including the barren lands. There was something about that place that drew me to it; even though it was the one place where I almost pooped my pants in front of a girl. Who would have known, I even had a yearning to visit the Academy, a place that some years back I was so desperate to leave. It was deserted when I visited. Classes were cancelled. The students were sent to areas of the Empire that needed aid. The Empire was having trouble containing the recent demon outbreaks.

Umaso and I were standing outside the massive facility that made up Atlas City's Intelligence headquarters. I was a bit nervous about seeing her. It had been so long since I had seen her face in the flesh. I was blushing with the thought of seeing that smile on her face. I noticed Umaso was more anxious than I, he didn't like waiting.

I saw Gaya approach from the distance. She was beautiful as ever. She looked radiant with her recent tan. Just the mere sight of her caused my internal body temperature to rise; I was sweating profusely; I was falling apart inside. I had to keep my cool.

"Jack!" she said from the distance as she approached smiling, her black eyes were shining. She stopped after taking a short, strange hop.

"How are you? Didn't you get here…" She looked to my side and noticed my company.

"Oh, this is Umaso, a friend from back in the Colony." She wasn't listening to me.

"Aiyoo…" She said softly. The shine of her eyes had vanished with her smile.

"Excuse me?" Umaso replied.

"You don't recognize me?" Gaya was hysterical. "It's me, Gaya!"

Umaso didn't reply. He was rather caught off guard more so than I. He was looking at her as if she was some lunatic who was having some schizophrenic attack.

"AIYOO" Gaya's eyes were full of tears as she yelled at the top of her lungs. She grabbed Umaso by the shoulders, shaking him in such desperate manner, almost as if she was crying for help. It was all very dramatic "What did they do to you?"

Gaya's face turned serious in a flash. She took a couple of steps back and drew out one of her swords. It was narrow, adorned in a way that it resembled an angel's wing; her first lover's memento. That sword, how could I have forgotten, there was only one other sword like that, one of Umaso's back up weapons.

I was shocked at this realization. The sweat in my forehead had gone cold, and I felt my heart sink.

"Aiyoo, when you gave me this… you promised me you'd never forget our promise! You said you'd find me no matter what." Gaya was bawling. "And you also said that if you ever forgot me, that one touch of this sword would bring you back."

Umaso, or Aiyoo if that's his real name, approached Gaya slowly. He reached his hand and touched Gaya's sword.

At that moment, Umaso started to grab his head, his eyes were forced shut. His face expressed pain as if he was getting his skull ripped apart. Umaso got down to his knees, hyperventilating. After a moment, he gave me a smile. Umaso barely ever smiled, and seeing him smile like that while looking at me felt very creepy

"Jackie, thanks to you I finally got my memories back."
Umaso said between breaths while looking at me with a
smile. He then turned his eyes to her. "Gaya, your boobs
grew."

Gaya smacked him in his balls. "You also said that if you
never contacted me I could beat you up, gives me the right."
She smiled and hugged him.

They didn't move for what seemed an eternity. I bet she had
been dreaming about this moment every day since they last
saw each other.

He closed his eyes and he said "You can't imagine how
happy I am to see you."

That was my line before this whole twist was thrown in my
face. I didn't know how to feel at the time.

Nearly two weeks passed since we had been released from
detainment.

Alon was stuck working in the mechanical department. The
increased demand was putting his duties ahead of his
personal issues. I could only imagine how desperate he was
getting. Sonja started to work in Alon's department. It was
only natural since Sonja was our resident *LCU* pilot and
mechanical expert. Of course that helped rise suspicion
about the activity of those two.

With Alon stuck with his orders, and with Umaso resting
while recovering his memories, there was not a whole lot I
could do about Sela. As for Gaya, her world had now
become Umaso. She spent as much time as she could
helping Umaso regain his memories. Since she had been
busy with Umaso, she asked me for help, so I had spent the
past days doing a lot of library research and paperwork for
Gaya. I didn't really want to, but I had to seem supportive
of the cause and suck it up. It really was a horrible moment
for me, doing paperwork with one arm was really a huge

handicap. Well, at least my "dead" arm was not stiff. It was malleable enough for me to pose it however I pleased.

The jealousy was making me go insane. I had dreamt of being with Gaya for years, to at least try kindling a spark between us, and now this. I couldn't understand why I was being such a selfish prick. It's the happy story of two friends, whose only desire was to be with each other -- Umaso being more recent -- , but more importantly, my own heart was split in two between her and Shamain; whom I desperately wanted to contact. I was in no right to want someone who had found her happiness with someone else.

Chapter 7 -- *a Bold Punkass Move*

The storm of chaos didn't stop with the demon--related incidents in the space frontier. I had to file numerous incidents of demon attacks. The earlier ones were on the furthest points from Atlas city. Then the attacks started to spring up inside the empire. First it was the rural areas, and then they moved into the major metropolises.

Doing Gaya's paperwork was driving me nuts. It took me a good while to get used to the demands of her job. Luckily, it was basic fill--in work, so it didn't require her expertise. It was the general recording information of incidents, criminal or demon related. It would have been very easy--going work, but the plethora of reports was piling in.

I couldn't help feel jealous about the whole Gaya--Aiyoo romance saga. I felt cheated, like the heavens were pulling a prank out of my ass. It was infuriating to think that I had been me the one to link these two in holy bullshit. And Gaya's love just HAD to be Umaso. He had become one of my closest friends, and I owed him my life a thousand times over. And at the same time, knowing that he was much more suited than me to be with Gaya, even without their history, just sunk my heart.

It is around this time when I started to feel my temper getting volatile; luckily I was on my own at the time for the most part. Just imagining what could have been with Gaya made my head boil. Then, when it came to Shamain, it was becoming a delicate balance of love and hate. It was around this time, the first time I noticed that something was taking over me. It was wanton desire coupled with a desire to hurt them, and being jealous of Umaso; it was killing me to think that way.

I had to get my head out of these broads. The idea of heading to the Southlands in search of Sela was becoming a very attractive idea.

Nobody dared go to the southern lands. Though the rise of the Hunter's empire managed to lower the threat of these lands, it was just too costly to maintain full control. Demons had long transformed the place into a wasteland. The lack of the empire's control had made this place a haven for fugitives. The constant demon incidents and criminals made my going there like a cuddly, innocent, delicious baby seal swimming in a sea of sharks.

Gaya and I were in her office. She was surrounded by her comfy office furnishings while I was sitting at a desk in the corner, like her little bitch. I was sunk in my funky mood for a while by then.

"Hey Jack, I am trying to fill in a report, but you have all the current information. Can you do it for me?" Doing Gaya's work had become routine, and there was no pay.

"Sure" I had yet to deny her. But this time, my voice had gone harsh that day.

"Are you ok?" She asked while she observed my expression, and then she snapped "You know, you don't have to do this if you don't want to. I can do it by myself."

Her snapping caught me by surprise. For a moment, I think I saw her show some guilt having me do her work ever since we met again. Maybe she wanted to spend more time with me, but circumstances got in the way…. But she snapped at me, so fuck it.

"Right, you know you can't do this without me." I snarled back.

She stared at me for a brief moment; her face was full of disbelief.

"What is wrong with you!" her face turned furious. "I don't want to talk to you if you're going to be like this."

"Then how the fuck should I talk to you, huh? Should I be your submissive bitch all the time?" I couldn't contain an evil smirk while I said it. It felt so good.

She turned her eyes away from me. She didn't say anything.

"Gaya…" I reached for her arm, but she brushed my hand away.

The bustling sound of the offices had turned silent. I had just over stepped on my boundaries, and I could just feel her disappointment fill the room. I wanted to say sorry, but I couldn't.

All I wanted was for her to see me as someone other than just her friend. Instead, I ended up hurting her at a level I never thought I'd be able to.

I grabbed her by the shoulders and tried drawing her close to me. I wanted to hug her, to tell her that I was sorry, but she tried pushing me away. In an instant of desperation, I grabbed her by the back of her neck, and forced my lips on hers.

As soon as I felt her lips, I knew I had messed up big time. I was expecting a violent reaction or no feedback at the least, but what followed was something that took me by surprise.

Her lips started to move with mine. I could never forget the softness of her lips; it was like kissing clouds -- if clouds could be kissed at all.

Her body relaxed and it moved with mine. Her hands were around the back of my head.

I felt my body was sinking into hers. But then I felt her push me, the thought of Umaso took over. I backed away.

"Sorry" I starred at her eyes for a moment, and then I stormed out.

Chapter 8 -- *Escape from Atlas*

I left her office as fast and as quietly I could to not call any attention.

The feeling of guilt was all over me as I was walking the streets to think what I should do next. What was more confusing to me was Gaya's response to my attack.

I felt terrible. I had ruined two of my closest friendships in one move. My embarrassment would not let me see them again after everything Umaso had done for me. I couldn't face anyone, but I didn't know what I should do... and then it hit me. I needed to leave Atlas city.

I couldn't tell Alon about my plan. His closeness to Sonja made it uncomfortable for me to confide on him.

I did, however, have to have a plan on where to go. An in an instance of inspiration, I found my calling. I was going to save Sela.

At the time I did not realize how ridiculous an idea it was. An imperial agent with a retarded arm walking into rebel territory... But I didn't care. This was my way to vindicate my own actions; trying to be the hero for once. I even had it all mapped out.

I would first step into my quarters, grab whatever supplies I could get, and then leave the city through the barren lands, where security was minimal. My military status would allow me to get past whatever check points there could be.

It was a zip. No problems getting to the city limits. I even stopped by an old bar before I left. I heard that ever since the incident where Gaya and I almost got killed a heavy cloud -- that same purple fog I was engulfed in-- formed over the barren lands after every sunset. No one had any concrete theories as to why; everything in the world was changing rapidly. The demonic aura made it impossible to cross it.

I had to risk it. I arrived a couple hours before dusk. I was planning to use Gaya's umbrella (the one that broke, I had repaired it); with it, if I hurried, I could make it out in a hurry.

I proceeded on foot until I made it into the lower part of the lands. And then I decided to fly low so that there were no chances of getting caught. Although it would be a time consuming process, I also had to play it safe. And it seemed to pay off.

That is until I was near the outside edge of the barren lands. The sun was setting deep in the horizon by the time I was halfway through the valley, and the fog took over the land. It wasn't too hard to fight off the aura. In fact, it was as though it was nourishing me with energy. I was even gaining some feeling from my retarded arm, but I wasn't sure if it was real, or if the fog had gained on me. But when I saw Shamain's silhouette in front of me I thought I had lost it.

The fog gave way to her. She was sitting on a rock like a little girl waiting for someone while playing with her *pet*.

Shamain had one of the rarest abilities abilities in the magic tree. This *pet* behaved like a living creature, but it was always under the control of the user. Most people would think that this was actually a real companion, and without the proper detection ability, no one could notice. But more than an actual pet, this magic skill was more closely resembled to puppetry. What made this kind of magic so rare was that it required for the user to transfer part of her soul into the puppet. Splitting the soul itself was a skill that the user had to be born with, and then develop. Shamain possessed a number of puppets. Her main offensive weapon was a dragon four times her size. It was quite a fearful thing, that thing did have the spirit of a dragon within.

"Isn't this a lovely view?" She said referring to the sunset. She let the dragon fly off

"It's the best view in the world" I replied. She paused, and her expression showed how not amused she was.

"It's like the sky is engulfed in a raging fire. And the purple mist -- so dark, deep like blood -- covers the land, beauty that hides its poison. It is so quiet here, so peaceful in its violence" that was Shamain, always speaking in her own style, strange yet captivating. Actually, I didn't care what she talked about, she could be saying gibberish, and I would still listen. She would always use her hands to mimic what she was saying, and I would always follow her fingers.

"What are you doing here?" I said, trying to act cool headed.

"Preparing for the next phase of operation for my organization's goals to destroy the Empire" she said in the calmest way.

She was lying; just to screw around with my head. I would later (much later) find out that the 'organization' she was talking about was the Empire itself.

I didn't expect to hear her tell me her 'secret' agenda, knowing that I am a soldier of the Empire. But what really struck me was her non--existent reaction to my presence. I was out of words for a moment. I was having trouble controlling my rage; I could feel my body tensing.

"Tell me then; what did you do to my arm?" I replied. "Why didn't you kill me that day? Don't I know too much about you?"

She gave me a nasty grin. "I kind of did you know. I left you to die -- hint, hint?" Her cold way of talking to me was hurting me just as much as back in space. And then her expression changed "But I am really glad you survived -- I think I would have missed you... And answer your question/s; it doesn't matter what you know, you won't do anything against me because you love me."

I wasn't sure if she was putting a spell on me because the words were escaping from my head. I clenched my throat, and held it in.

"Of course I love you." I said "But then why did you just leave like that?"

She shrugged, already annoyed.

"I've thought about what you told me that day; about a power inside me." I stopped; she didn't seem to be listening to me. "Can you at least explain this?" I said while I was pointing at my arm.

She got down of her rock and approached me in quite a seducing manner. She walked until she was a small step away from me; when I thought she was going to stop, she leaned on as if to kiss me -- lips and all. I instinctively leaned towards her; my heart was beating like a machine gun. She then faked away, with a grin. "Too easy" she muttered.

"Actually, I was waiting for you here." She said after a brief moment of silence.

"Why is that?"

"I don't know anymore. I am thinking whether if I should kill you or let you live." She said "Anyways, I'm out. I've got other things to do."

"Shamain, please" I cried in desperation while I grabbed her wrist in a rush.

She didn't pull back, but she didn't turn around either. I let her arm go.

"Whatever it is that you're doing; if you want me to, I will go with you." I said. "You can always consider me as your friend. I mean, you don't have to do this alone."

"Who says I'm alone; as if I needed you for anything!" She yelled.

I was out of words. I didn't know what in the world I could have said to make her understand my feelings.

"You can't do anything for me." She said calmly. "I am going to destroy this current empire; that means that a lot of your friends could be dying on the process. Are you willing to murder your own friends?"

"I didn't think of it that way…"

"Exactly, you don't think much." Shamain hissed. "Anyways…"

"You don't have to do this Shamain." I said, trying to get my thoughts together.

"Oh really, and then what, let this world be ruled by the discriminating rule of this empire?! Have you not seen with your own eyes how the vast majority of the people live, or are you so stuck living in your own ways that you can't see it" She said "Grow up."

"I am not saying this empire is a perfect one, but why are you with an organization that plans to kill millions of people to achieve their supposed goal of peace" I retracted "I don't know what kind of group you belong to, but by the looks of it that is the kind of organization you're in. I understand your motives, but there has to be a better way."

I took a pause, trying to control myself. "I don't know how, but I'll find a way to fix this world. If that is what you want to do I will help you" I said "Come with me, you don't have to be doing things like this."

"What makes you think that I don't want to do things this way?"

"Because you're too good of a person" I said without thinking much about my words.

Her face expression changed for a moment.

"Do you always talk like a child?" She replied. "Do you know why the empire separates the children from their parents? It is because the empire does not want its population to find out the truth of their own past. All the things the history books and the legends say about the Mighty Hunter are nothing but a twist from the truth."

"I don't follow, what are you saying?" I said, confused by the news.

"That arm, no, you hold the key to a legacy of past ages." She said "I can take that key from you, but if I did, I would end up killing you."

"Then why don't you kill me?" I said without realizing at the time that it was my life she was talking about.

She paused for a moment. "I can't. Because I consider you my friend; I just can't seem to go through it."

She walked towards me, and she slowly put her arms around me.

"I will be seeing you soon." She said

"Where are you going? Why don't you come with me? You don't have to do this alone…" I said while holding her tightly.

"You ask too many questions." She said softly "Here, I am about to show you."

"Shamain, don't go. Whatever it is..." I didn't get to finish my words. I guess Shamain had a knack to sweep me off my feet.

When I woke up, I almost shit myself when I saw the most terrifying monster I had ever seen. I wanted to run away, but my body gave no reaction. I then realized that it wasn't my body.

It was as though my mind had been transferred into someone else's body. I was watching the world through someone else's eyes. I could even hear his thoughts, and I could sense everything through him. It took me a moment to remember that the last thing that happened before I woke up in this scenario was Shamain's words '... I am about to show you.' Great, she had placed me under another spell. Nice way to treat someone you call a friend.

Chapter 9 -- *The Hero of the Sword*

It was the Mighty Hunter's spear what drove the fatal blow
to the monstrous beast that night. But it was his younger
brother, the Hero of the Sword, the one that stood up the
longest against the demon while carrying his brethren with
him. That is one of the things I was about to find out shortly
while being inside him… it does sound slightly strange
writing that.

When everything seemed lost for the tribe of men, the Hero
of the Sword stood valiantly against the indomitable beast.
Man and demon stood there for a brief moment which
seemed an eternity. The hero knew this was it. His legs
were starting to fail him; the weapon he was carrying
seemed to have doubled in weight. He had difficulty
breathing, and his sight was getting blurry. The beast in
front of him was mangled and covered in blood. Its breath
stunk of rotten corpses.

The sun was starting to set.

This dream spell that Shamain placed me under was a little
bit too good. I could really feel everything. The body I was
in felt like it was weakening; the pain and fatigue was
enough that it would make me collapse. Breathing was very
shallow, and taking in air was painful; the vision was getting
blurry. The hero had injuries all over his body. I could feel
how the blood was flowing out of him, and the pain was just
too strong and too real. I didn't understand how this man
could still be standing and wielding such a heavy sword.

The sword he was wielding was almost as big as him. The
blade had a faint glow of white to it despite the noticeable
battle damage. The guard on the sword was beautifully
ornate with angels.

The hero was now down to a knee.

'This spell dreams feels a little bit too real; did I really have to feel pain in my crotch, too?!' I complained

'What was that?' the hero's thought came shouting out. *'It must be some sort of demonic power from this beast. I am starting to hear strange voices in my head. Come on, I must not give up..."*

'Did he just hear me? What kind of spell is this? People aren't supposed to hear you in a dream spell'

'What spell is this that you are talking about. You must be an imp under the beast's command. Leave now before I crush you after I'm done with your master.'

'I am no little demon. I am a human being... I just don't understand why I am answering to you; this is just a dream.'

'You said this is a dream? I wish it was.' The hero's mind went blank for a moment *'Maybe you're the soul of my fallen comrades whose soul is trapped inside a spell. Do not worry my brother. I will rescue you from this foul beast!'*

'What? No, no. I am not a demon or some weird trapped soul or whatever you think I am. It may be hard to grasp, but I come from the future.'

'The future, what kind of a future is this?'

'Well --assuming this is all real-- I come from a time years after the legendary beast is defeated, and people live in peace. Demons are no longer the threat it used to be.'

'Ah, that is good to hear. You must be a messenger sent from the heavens then.'

So he now thinks I'm sent from heaven. I never imagined that one of the most significant figures of history to be this dense, but to his credit the power of his will was almost unlimited.

I could feel everything the hero of the sword could. Ever since I had woken up inside him -- that sounds strange -- the hero of the sword was giving up.

As soon as he finished those words, it was as if I had been transported to a completely new body. The pain was gone, and the hero's vision was now focused on the target. His mind was blank. There were no thoughts on combat strategy; there was nothing.

The warrior readied his sword in front of him in preparation for one last strike. The warrior charged towards the beast. The demon gave out a massive roar while it stood on its hind legs.

"Brother!" The hero gave out a roar of his own and rushed towards his opponent who was now very close.

In an instant, the beast swung its massive left arm at the warrior. The hero used the flat side of the blade to deflect the blow; he guided the sword forward, turned his torso, and extended his right arm and drove the sword into the beast through its throat.

The beast gave another, stronger, deafening roar.

The demon swung its claws at the hero, who could not dodge this attack. Next thing I could see was the hero was thrown in the ground, with his right arm missing. The rest of his arm still had a grip on the sword.

One of the claws was hooked deep inside the hero's right shoulder. I could feel the pain govern the hero's body. The warrior's strength was gone.

Behind the beast stood another warrior armed with a long spear with the same glow as the hero's sword. Though he looked battered from battle, he had a strong presence about him. When the hero launched his last strike on the beast, this warrior rushed the demon from behind while its focus was on the hero. He drove his spear from behind to the base of the beast's skull. The Mighty Hunter had given the fatal flow to the beast.

'My angel,' that was my strange new name *'please tell me about this future that you speak of.'* I felt his mind was in a state peace I had never felt before.

''Well, according to history books, after the legendary beast gets defeated; we humans made use of the gift from the heavens. People used this ethereal energy that would later become the foundation of the empire that I live in. Yes, the human civilization is governed as one single nation. The Mighty Huntert managed to find peace among people in the world.''

"I see, you really are an angel. So the sacrifice made this day will bring forth a world where demons don't exist anymore. My brothers, we did it."

"Well, actually, demons still exist in my world. But thanks to our ability to use ethereal energy, we were given a weapon that has made people the rulers of the earth. The Mighty Hunter built a kingdom by his own hand, and today marks the birth of his reign. Lately, there has been an increased activity by demons."

I thought that the warrior would be feeling something similar to ecstatic about the great news, but instead his heart felt heavy and torn.

"You've really messed your shit up this time," said the Mighty Hunter with a smile while extending his hand to the warrior. "You saved us all"

"How many of us are left?" the Hero asked.

"It's just you, I and the ones who got sent back brother, and our eldest was the first one to go down. Do you think that you'll make it?"

"Maybe, help me get this claw off my shoulder," the hero said as he sat up with his brother's help. I asked him to just lie down because the simple act of sitting up caused 'us' to feel a stinging pain in the whole body, but he ignored me.

56

The Hunter nursed his brother's wounds with cloths and various herbal creams.

After the Hunter bandaged the beaten warrior, they sat in their spots. They reflected on what had taken place in between moments of meditation. There was an herbal soothing sensation in his skin; it went rather well with the theme of that moment. I couldn't feel the right half of my host's body.

"Brother" The hero of the sword broke silence for one last time. "Where will we go from here on?"

"We have the blessing from the heavens now, we can do anything, and we can go anywhere. With this new power we can conquer this world under heaven's name. Had it not been for your valiant sacrifice, we wouldn't be standing in triumph."

"If you see it that way, it was thanks to our eldest when he cut the beast's tail, reducing its strength in half." He paused, and changed his tone "but brother, what do you mean by your words? What is this new determination of yours? You are the second eldest, so I know I am disrespecting you by questioning your motives, but please stop"

"I understand your concern brother. I tried to reason my ideals to our eldest, and just like you, he was closed to any other possibilities. But think, with the power that allows us to to take down the strongest demon lord in this earth; we can use it to destroy all demons in this earth.
"This new gift that we have is not just limited to our weapons. I got this idea when I spoke to one of your now fallen brothers. He studied the land on this mountain, and he noted that the materials from this land resonate with our swords; meaning that we can make more weapons that we can use.
"Just imagine the countless possibilities that lay ahead for our children, we can bring forth a new era with heaven in our backs!

"If our brother's observation is correct, then we can create a new world. Please brother, let's at least give this a try. If this doesn't work, then we can still fulfill our mission."

The warrior stopped and spoke to me for a brief moment.

'My angel, are you still there?'

'I am not 'your' angel, and yes I am still here'

'I finally got it; you said you come from the future, right? And with everything else you've told me, it means that my brother's plans come to fruition. People learn how to use the power that belongs to demons.'

'You could say that.'

'People even learn how to travel back in time. With a power like that...'

'I didn't really come here by my own will. I don't really know..."

Before I could finish my words --for just a moment-- the hero's mind had gone to see an incredibly beautiful woman. Her hair was wavy, and it had erogenous smell. The hero's feelings shook me to the core. I fell in love with her.

'... She is beautiful. Sorry, but your feelings for her are very strong'

'I know; it's ok. How not to love her? But I won't be able to see her again. The sun will not rise for me. You can feel it right? I've lost too much blood, and the poison is spreading quickly.'

I could barely feel his body anymore.

"Brother, help me stand up."

The Hunter helped him get up. The Hero of the Sword then walked towards his sword. After removing his right hand out of the way, he held his sword.

"Brother, this obsessive path that you've chosen will only lead you to misfortune. I won't be able to make it this time. Think of your brothers who have laid their lives for our mission. It is our dying wish, honor our death. Please, for me, the one related to you by blood."
"I am sorry"

"Even if you had to kill me, you'd still do it?"

The Hunter didn't answer.

'Our oldest brother told me that with this new power, as long as we hold our holy arm, we can do anything. Having had you with me; makes me really believe it. I will try and heal my wounds.' He paused to concentrate.

'Ok, that didn't work. But somehow I feel as though my spirit is moving towards my sword. You can feel it too, right?'

'Yes, that is how my generation uses ethereal energy. We channel it through our tools, or weapon in this case.'

I started questioning how quickly he got to comprehend the use of his abilities. I had a suspicion that he too could get inside my own thoughts. I felt exposed. But moving one's own spirit was something that I had never heard of.

In his last moments, the Hero of the Sword was standing next to the fallen demon lord. His rags were getting stained in blood. He grieved as he looked at his brother. He tightened his grip on his sword. He turned, and in a sudden move, he impaled his sword against the beast.

Before I realized, the hero had been skewered by the Hunter's spear from the back. I didn't feel a thing.

'Damn, I missed. I am sorry. You've been a good companion, but now I must entrust you with my own mission. I can't do it. You have to destroy the Demon King's jewel. It is the only way to eradicate demons from entering this world.'

I was out of words. Everything that I witnessed through the hero's eyes; to find out that he just now entrusted me with a mission that could change the world, and to see that the man whom I had read about to be the founder of the empire was able to murder his own brother… I was afraid. All I could say was *'yes'*.

I felt the warrior's life fade away as he was trying to lift his sword again. Then I lost connection with the warrior.

Chatper 10 -- *The Bill*

This has little to do with the events ahead.

Before I made my escape from Atlas, I decided to visit an old venue that I used frequent when I was still enrolled in the Academy. Alon, Sela, and I used to go there for drinks. It was called *The Bill.* Alon and Sela were friends with the owner, so we always got into the VIP room. But this time we just sat at the bar. The music was playing, and there were a lot of girls dancing that night.

I didn't really liked going out much because I would get some massive hangovers the next day, and I was usually the one who got hammered the most.

It was the usual trio: Sela, Alon, and me. We were just chatting and reminiscing about our life together through all these years. Sela would occasionally bring out the number of beasts he took out over Alon, and Alon would retaliate by bragging on how Sela had never beaten him in machines racing, and to add salt to the wounds, Alon mentioned that I had beaten him in a race. I had beat Sela once, but I had won accidentally the first time we raced because I didn't know how to brake.

Eventually Sela got up to talk to a girl. I never understood how he did it, but it went something like:

'Why is such a beautiful girl such as you out here all on her own?' he would say.

'Oh, nothing, I just came here to see what you were up to?' the girl would reply, blushing and horny.

It was easy for him to talk to these girls. And yes, it was a bit corny most of the time, but it worked for him. I had tried using one of his lines, and I ended up getting a rather hostile response.

We had been drinking heavily that night. Alon kept pushing me drinks all night. I got so drunk I tried to pick up a girl on my own, and I got turned down badly. One of them almost tried to hit me. Everyone laughed at me, even my friends. So I went back to sit down.

"Ok, calm down. No more drinks for you" Alon said that as he handed me another drink.

We kept drinking. I don't know how much time had passed by already, but I was really drunk by then. Alon knew that.

"So, how are things between you and Gaya?" Alon asked casually.

"Pretty good" I replied "she makes me buy her a lot of food. I even gained a couple pounds."

"Oh, good, good" Alon paused "Are you two dating now?"

"No, we're just friends. I know; it's a bit strange since I never used to talk to her." I replied.

"So, do you have some feelings for her?" I didn't say anything for a moment. What could I have said? Even I wasn't sure if I liked Gaya.

"It's ok" Alon continued "We all know you like her, and I think she likes you, too. Judging by how she is around you and all. I know her and she is your type of girl"

I didn't know what to think of Alon's lines. I wasn't sure why he was encouraging me to be going out with Gaya.

"Well, yeah, I guess I should ask her." I replied. My face was feeling very warm.

"Ha! So you do like her!" Sela barged in. I was too drunk to tell anything anyways. "Hey Alon, all this time Jackie over here was worried that he was backstabbing you."

"Dumbass" He replied with a smile.

"Well, sorry." I couldn't talk anymore. The alcohol had soaked through all of my body.

Right on that moment, four guys came into the bar. They were a bit older than us, and they looked rather hostile. They noticed us.

One of them asked "Aren't you kids from the academy?"

"Yes we are! Do you want a drink?" I replied.

"We don't like your kind around here, so better get going" the same person continued.

"I don't think so. Why don't you go back to beating up your wives because I bet they're the only ones who can stand you; unless you're looking to get your well deserved ass kicking?" Alon was not the type to give in. His eyes were turning real red.

The four men were getting ready "What did you say!"

"Go home…" I tried to continue, but instead I started to take a nap.

"Your ears don't seem to be working right, let me fix them for you." As soon as Sela said that, he landed a punch into the face of the guy in the front.

The next three guys tried to rush in, but Alon greeted one with a foot. One of the guys grabbed a bottle and swung it at Sela's head. Sela dodged. Alon gave that one a sweet hook in the jaw. The last guy tried to rush Sela, but the guy tripped and landed on the floor, face first.

All four of the guys were in the floor. Sela and Alon then proceeded to kick them in the floor. They didn't get back up again. By the time Sela and Alon were done with them, the four hostiles were quite macerated.

We left as soon as the fight finished. While I was being dragged by Sela, the two were laughing and talking about

63

the fight. In my mind, I would ask Gaya out.. but by the next morning, all bravery from alcohol had worn off.

But my favorite event at The Bill was my graduation night. The same night after Gaya had left town. I was quite unhappy about her leaving. Since I was about to leave to Colony twenty two, I didn't know when I would see her again. Then I met this girl named Numid. She was a non *ethereal* user who had just come into town.

For the longest time, I couldn't remember much of her face, but she had some juicy lips as if they were full of nectar. And her tongue had the dexterity of a surgeon. I remember we were talking a bit. Just general questions such as "what do you do for fun," or "what is your favorite food." There was a very awkward moment of silence. At that moment I reached for her hand, and the next thing I know, we were making out --for hours. That is how my first kiss went.

This last time I visited The Bill. I saw Numid again. I didn't know she had started working there since we met. I didn't really talk to her after that night we kissed. Her black curls and those big brown eyes and that creamy chocolate skin of hers; how could have I forgotten that face?

There werent any other customers so she sat next to me. We spoke again, this time the silence was much more awkward than before. When she got close enough, I leaned to kiss her. This time I reached under her shirt and pants. I will always remember her ass. It was hard like steel, just delicious.

We went to the back of the bar. The storage closet was big enough to house a small bed. It was the first time I had the pleasure of experiencing intercourse. And I sucked. I wasn't counting, but I know I didn't last past three minutes.And my member was not reaching maximum hardness. Soon after, I went two more times; still lasted less than three minutes. To make it worse, I couldn't maintain full erection. I blame it on the alcohol. But maybe it was also because her girlfriend was nearby, watching.

I was rather disappointed; not only by my performance, but the whole experience of sex in itself. All that time I had thought of sex to be something more magic. I stopped being a virgin inside that closet in all ways -- she stuck a finger up my butt.

Regardless, Numid was a very kind towards me. We didn't speak much, but she took my under her bossom. I had contemplated at the idea of staying a couple of days with Numid before I went to face Gaya again, but then an unfortunate event happened.

I was sitting next to Numid inside the closet while drinking liquor when we heard some customers come in. I heard some familiar voices. I peeked to see who it was. It was Alon, and he brought Sonja, Gaya, and Umaso. How dare him. I tried to remain hidden while Numid went to serve out.

"I feel a familiar presence." Gaya said.

Huh, lucky me. In normal circumstances Gaya would have known I was nearby with her sensory skills. My only theory is that she could not immediately tell it was me because I had just had sex. That is the best analysis I could come up with; its either that or she just pretended it wasn't me. I snuck out of that place as fast and silently I could.

Chapter 11 -- *Ground Cycle Journey*

My entire right shoulder all the way up to my neck was cramped up. I couldn't turn my head. Shamain left me to lie in the most uncomfortable position it seemed. That and I had a raging headache like someone had hammered nails into my skull.

The sun was high up in the sky. I have no idea how long I had been out for. I tried using Gaya's umbrella, but it was busted. No idea what happened to it, maybe it was the fog. Waking up after witnessing such a strange dream or whatever it was left me slightly confused. Leaving Atlas city and escaping the mess I had just made was not the crucial objective it had been the day before.

The only person I could turn to, as I saw it, was Sela. The problem was that I had no idea how to get to him. I figured I would head south; besides, I couldn't return just yet -- not sure why I thought of it that way.

I had walked several hours, and I already doubted myself. The sweat in my ass was starting to get very uncomfortable. I decided I would make a pit stop on the next town; no way that I could make it all the way by foot.

I was drenched in sweat; even I knew it was time to get a shower. I made the stop at the next town I could reach. Although it was a day and a half's distance away, the location felt very different from Atlas. The place seemed rather primitive in its infrastructure.

On my short stay I was able to make a deal with a local shop. I bought an old Leatonian ground cycle. It had that vintage feel to it, so it caught my eye from the start. I know I got scammed on the transaction. The seller saw that I was rather desperate for a ride, and seeing that I was from the capital he charged me a fortune; the bastard, he made me give up my telecom trinket on the deal. After buying some more supplies, I ended up spending all of my savings.

Although I had installed a new Leatonian crystal, the damn thing was still very slow. I would take me an entire moon cycle before I could reach the borders of the southern regions. Still, travelling by ground, feeling the cycle move through the terrain was quite liberating.

There were times when I would get stuck due to bad terrain, whether it was mud or even massive sink holes that called for detours that would delay me for a day. The roads on the region were not really maintained at all. Whatever passable facilities were just remnants of a failed project by the empire to civilize the south. It got worse the further I travelled. At least it was a sign that I was headed in the right direction.

As I passed the last remaining town -- it was much more primitive than the first town I was in; people there did not seem to be well off either -- I came to realize how far I had travelled. I had never seen people struggling so much just to live. People looked at me with fear and resentment; I had never experienced that before. This was the world that Shamain had told me about. I left that post as soon as I restocked on my supplies.

I spent the nights on the open. Waking up was a pain, literally. Every morning I was greeted with a refreshed stiff neck on top of the whiplash from the day before. I was surprised my neck did not have the same fate as my dumb arm. And though the idea of sleeping in the open sounded romantic when I first thought of it; in reality, I would nearly piss myself every night in fear of demons. Nights felt much louder than days thanks to the disturbing howls I would hear coming from the darkness. And I always had a sense that some demons were following me.

It wasn't all bad though. During those days, there was a predominant feeling of freedom. And I had a lot of time to think about everything.

That dream/spell Shamain placed me. I still wasn't sure what it was all about. If it was all true, then it meant that my innate ability was to time travel, but it could just mean that it was Shamain's ability. And I was still not sure as to why I have this stoned arm. I kept regretting not having asked her why my arm was this way, what did she want with me or whatever it was that she saw in me? I just hoped to see her again, maybe then she wouldn't be so impossible.

Hell, if I had such a unique power, then the Empire had known about my abilities since my birth. Thinking that way, it would finally make sense how I managed to enter the Academy with my sub--par abilities. But then, why had the Empire officials had not kept a closer eye on me. Exactly how was Shamain involved in all this? What the fuck was this key she mentioned?

At times I wondered about the Hero of the Sword. That instance was all too real for it to be a farce. Moreover, if it was all true, then the use of ethereal energy was never supposed to be used the way it had been used throughout this dynasty. If I took in consideration the mysterious appearance of demons, then it would mean that ethereal ores and the power they had was linked to the demonic world, and not to the heavens -- shit was really going down.

The Hero placed in me a duty that would involve changing the entire world as I knew it. How in the world could I ever do such a thing? The irony of someone like me to have such a responsibility made me laugh; it was just too ridiculous.

I came to realize that the wraith I faced at the barrens some years ago could have been the Hero of the sword.

I built countless scenarios in my mind on how I would approach the mess I made with Gaya and Umaso/Aiyoo. In all of them, I end up getting my ass beat by Umaso. Hell, sometimes Gaya was the one to lay the pain in my behind. But to me, it was all unfair. How, why, did the girl I claimed to have such feelings for have to be destined to one of my best friends, and all I was supposed to do is keep quiet. Sometimes I felt this fortune of mine was all bullshit.

Then there is Shamain, to whom I wasn't sure if my feelings were true or if they were some spell/curse that she placed me on -- and may I add, she had already rejected me every single time I asked her out, with zero hesitation. It really hurt me to see that she was someone that I cared for to no end, and I could not do anything. I felt a connection with her that I had only experienced a few times -- and it had never been this strong. And no matter how much I wanted to reach to her, none of my willpower made a difference.

What does it take for two people to love each other unconditionally? The whole concept of love, the more I thought about it, the less sense it made. I had meditated upon this topic many nights over the period of many years (all my years). Despite appearances, it was not common for me to build feelings for just anyone, but that was irrelevant. In my experience, it didn't seem to matter how much a connection or kindred I had with any of these girls.

Really, it didn't matter what I did or said. It didn't matter if we liked the same movies. It didn't matter if we had a similar sense of humor -- well, we didn't match on the fart jokes, but everything else we did. It didn't matter how much time I spent helping her with whatever. It didn't matter if I could sit there listen to her talk for hours and really pay attention, or how beautiful she was to me in every way. It didn't matter if we liked our eggs the same way -- sunny side up with a pinch of pepper.

How on earth did I always end up going through these long runs chasing them, I have no clue. I didn't really spend my days envying my friends, but with Sela, that guy had a much easier time with girls. They just flocked to him. Well, he had a much different appearance than me. He was taller, bigger, he was built, and most anything he did, he did it well. That and he had that mysterious vibe to him with the demons and all. The difference was clear. He would use these lines, they were as simple as "excuse me miss, what is a beautiful girl like you doing here without her company," and that would be it. He would say those things back in the Academy days; I tried emulating him when I was at Colony twenty--two. It didn't work for me.

But comparing me to Sela wasn't really fair; he was on a different level. Besides, I had to take into account that they chose to spend their time with me, not someone else, and as I recall, they had plenty of choices. No, the reason why they could not, or would not, have that kind of feeling towards me was something else, and it was actually rather simple. I was about to learn that lesson shortly.

Chapter 12 -- *Jackie rises above Four*

Sela had a different upbringing from me. Like other half--breeds, he wasn't born with the same 'privileges' that I had. He was brought up in a small town where people like him were placed in. Because of his family's *nobility* --being a descendant of the Priestess of Light and all-- he was brought up with some wealth. But the root of his blood was something that placed him under scrutiny by the Empire and its mercy. At least he got to know his parents.

Aiyoo and Gaya grew up on the Eastern continent, where they grew up together. And from what I gathered, Shamain's west island was not a paradise.

Once Sela hit age, he was drafted into the Academy due to his innate abilities. That is when I met him. Although we lived in the same building, he kept to himself and the few other half--breeds, and me being my reserved self, we didn't really talk. That was until years later that he found out that I was known for being decent at trap setting in *demon purge* excursions. It was the least demanding position in terms of ethereal channeling, but it made placed the *setter* as the demon's main target nine out of ten times. I teamed up with him one time, and after that our friendship took off.

Demon purging, or demon hunting, was one of the perks that came from being in the Academy. A student had the choice to enroll in they were interested. The demon hunting 'club' was more like a paramilitary group. It was a sport that involved a small team of 'hunters' that would be sent off to a remote location to deal with a demon possession -- with that said, demon hunting was also the leading cause of student casualties.

There was no reason to not join. Demon purging was the biggest source of entertainment in the empire. At the academy, it really helped being good at the hunts. It helped getting that sex appeal and gaining popularity. Now, the

problem with being a *setter* was the least attractive role --
with good reason, the setter is the walking bait of the team.
Hunters in the pro leagues were huge celebrities and the
champion knights of the Empire. They dealt with demon
cases instead of regular imperial officers. They fought off
incredibly strong monsters; cities plagued overrun by
demon--zombies; and even organized groups of demons.
Sela was a rising star -- he did it mostly to get women.

I had gotten to know Sela rather well in a short period of
time. One day he said:

"Jackie, we're brothers now. Despite you being quite
useless, and I being as awesome as I am I know I can count
on you when it matters."

He then handed me a three--pronged comb. It was encrusted
with tiny jewels at the rim; the ornament of the artifact gave
out its age.

"This is a memento that has been passed down by
generations in my family. Ideally, I'd give it to a girl, but I
feel like giving it to you instead. This comb is an artifact
that is linked to my bloodline. It is said that 'when the two
that belong together need to find each other, this comb will
guide them together with silk threads.' If anything happens,
you'll know how to find me. I know you love me man."

I felt very awkward and uncomfortable when he gave me his
comb.

After that day I had kept that comb in my BES. I was
camping out for the night when I decided to pull out the
comb sice I was not sure how to find Sela -- yes, I
remembered the whole comb deal in the midst of my
journey. I held it against the moon while I was examining it
when I noticed a thin hair -- it was not silk-- appearing out of
one of the prongs. This hair was long and it pointed straight
into one direction. No matter where I positioned the comb,
it would always point to that same spot. It was my clue.

My ground cycle was starting to fall apart as I ventured further south. The terrain was starting to get extremely hostile, so I was covering less ground each day. Days were extremely hot and humid, and the air felt heavy, similar to the fog in the barrens near Atlas. But nights were getting even worse. I could feel demons breathing down my neck, and on top of that I was being harassed by hungry bugs. I was starting to run short of my food and water supply with no place to restock, so I decided to start eating the damn insects myself. It was a battle I was progressively losing though.

I kept close watch to my surroundings. I rode close to mountain profiles in order to keep a low profile. I had to watch out for demons, criminals and anti--imperialist groups had taken the region as their home, and I was easy pickings if someone caught sight of me. The clothes I was wearing screamed Empire soldier. I being the moron that I am forgot to bring a change of clothes for after I left Atlas's limits. Oh yeah, I hadn't bathed in a long while.

It had been a little over three months since I made the losing deal on my cycle. I had woken up that morning with a new record on neck pain. I could not move my neck at all. After a quick bug hash I set to continue on my journey. My head was stuck at an angle so I had to see everything at a diagonal.

I checked my map. I had been two weeks since I crossed the location that was pointed out as the place where the Priestess of Light resided over a thousand years ago. I hadn't realized that I passed the landmark since according to the tale; it was an area where water still ran clear. I was hoping to be close to where the Priestess had faced the entity of a hundred thousand demons --the incident that ended up killing her.

It had been some hours past zenith, the sun was facing west. I entered through a path that was walled by rocky cliffs on both my sides. I was aware that I could be easily ambushed, but I decided to take the risk. Besides, it was not like I could see much on my sides thanks to my neck. The shade that

that cliff offered was welcome as well, the sun was merciless. I had turned many shades of dark by the constant exposure to the sun.

I made a sharp turn, when I suddenly got covered by a heavy cloud of smoke. I could not see past my nose. I noticed by the smell that it was a smoke bomb. I had come this far, only to be caught by bandits. I was more pissed off about my moronic decision to take this route than anything else.

Though I could not see; my immediate decision was to make a quick one eighty. It was by best chance to escape. I will blame this on poor visibility. I overshot my turn and ended up riding straight into a rock at full throttle.

My legs were the first to lift off the bike. I lost my sense of balance so I don't know what happened until my back hit the wall flat. Then my head hit the ground. I lost my sight for a brief moment. As I lay prostrated, I noticed the cycle was ten paces away from me. Just how far I flew, I have no idea.

I tried to get up as quickly as I could though I was feeling wobbly from the impact. I set my BES in suit up mode. Two custom hand cannons appeared on my right hip. One of them was mine, and the other one I got as a graduation present from Sela. The latter one was a little too powerful for me to use regularly. My personal shield, which was originally on my left arm, was mounted on my right. My trusty short lightweight sword, of about a forearm's length, was placed on my lower back. It was the same sword I had used against the sword--wielding wraith at the barrens. My gear vest had two explosive traps and an ethereal combat knife. I also had a boot knife.

The smoke cleared up, and I could make up the stage formed by an organized demon gang. My cycle was ten paces behind me. There was a demon zombie twenty paces straight ahead of me with a demon dog on his side. Two others were approaching my flanks. Behind him there was a bigger demon zombie, the alpha. They looked very human. They did not have any open wounds or signs of decay like the ones at the space colony. I wasn't sure how, but I had to assume I was facing an experienced group; which made them all the more dangerous.

'Don't worry if you lose your temper under pressure; you'll just die.' Those were the encouraging words that Umaso said to me often. I had to see this through no matter what.

My hand cannons had one shot before it had to be recharged for three minutes -- the number changes on different weapons depending on design and personal abilities. I had modified mine to have two shots. Sela's cannon had only one shot, but it had tremendous power. My plan of action was to take out the leader first. Sela's gift was the ace up my sleeve. I pulled out Sela's cannon with no hesitation. I steadied my aim; I took a deep breath, when I exhaled I pulled the trigger. The flash from the shot covered my view. A loud thunderous bang echoed through the rock walls. I felt the wind blowing my clothes, and the shockwave made my teeth hurt. I missed.

I don't know how that was possible even to this day. At the distance they were, and with the wide blast of the shot, there is no way I should have missed. But I did.

I took a couple of steps back. My next genius plan was to get on the cycle and flee. The demon zombie on the front signaled his dog to attack. The beast caught up with me in no time. It lunged at me, and its fangs were aimed at my throat. I didn't have enough time to draw my sword. I raised my right arm and manage to make the dog bite into my shield. The force of the dog knocked me to the ground. Its claws were tearing at me, and its jaw was crushing my shield. In a moment of panic I released my shield, and I reached for the combat knife in my vest. I stabbed the demon on the neck, and I kicked it. I cast a remote destruction spell through the knife -- a trick that had become my own staple ever since I learnt it. The dog was dead.

"You killed my fucking dog! I am going to enjoy tearing your little asshole apart." The zombie in the middle roared as he showed his teeth, his body was flexing to the point of tearing his skin.

The demon zombie charged at me along with the two flanking me.

The one on the right jumped me first. I rolled to my left, and I drew my gun as I got up. The zombie on the left was close enough to take a swing at me. I shot from my hip. The shot landed on his jaw, his head blew up, killing him. I was about to shoot the flanker from the right when the one on the middle tackled me hard enough to push me all the way to my cycle. I lost my gun.

My left arm should have broken, but seemed like my petrified arm was hard enough to take the hit. I took out both of my traps. I accidentally dropped one in the cycle's engine, my hand was shaking uncontrollably. I didn't have time to pick it back up so I threw the next one five paces in front of me, where I had calculated the zombies would be stepping on. As they were charging at me, I activated it. The middle zombie was knocked to the ground. The right flanker dodged it. I drew my sword as I charged. I swung the sword with a vertical strike, splitting his head in the middle. I then turned to execute the one on the ground.

I ran back to my cycle as I felt the leader was making his move. I hit the throttle to the max as I pumped my own energy into the cycle ready to joust the beast. I maneuvered to the left, but the zombie caught on to my move, and stopped the cycle with his bare hands. I once again was airborne. I lobbed past the zombie. Mid air I detonated the trap in the cycle, killing the leader. Those were the longest thirty seconds of my life.

I stayed on the ground gasping for some air. At that moment I didn't know if any of the zombies were still alive or if there were any more, but I didn't have anything left on my tank. When I got up to check I was in disbelief of what I had just accomplished.

I don't know what had got into me. I was afraid to no end, and I felt the pressure of the moment; this time I had no Sela or Umaso or Gaya backing me up. Yet, it was a moment of total concentration; I had never felt something like that.

I picked up whatever I could. My sword, combat knife, and both of my hand cannons were good. My ground cycle had been blown to pieces along with the zombie lead. Among the debris I found two more hand cannons. One had been broken on the explosion, but the other one was still working. I noticed the weapon had been fired just recently. It was a disturbing finding. Only those aligned with ethereal energy could make the cannons work. Even if the original body was that of an ethereal user, once a demon takes over, that ability is broken. I just had to be glad that the zombie missed.

I scouted their trail to see where their camping site may have been. I had all my weapons recharged, and ready. After an hour of tracking I couldn't pin point where they may have been. I figured that at least there were not any more demons.

When I landed on that final move, I fell on my knee with all my weight. The adrenaline wore off, and my knee felt like it was about to explode. My back was feeling incredibly sore, and so were my sides. It was uncomfortable to breathe. I had to stop and tend to my knee the best I could, but it was bruised pretty badly. Parts of my body were colored in many dark shades of purple.

Without the cycle, chances of finding Sela were now gone. I checked the priestess' comb, it pointed to the same location, but it didn't tell me how far away. With all my resources wearing thin, I had no hope of keep searching for Sela or even making it back home. It felt strange to come to the realization that I could be dying shortly. Though my trip to the south lands was as reckless as it could get, I never really thought about the risk of death. After I let reality sink in, I was over come by a feeling of determination that I'd do my best to survive, and that if death came, I would accept it with no regrets.

I tried to get away as far as possible from the fight scene; still following the direction the comb pointed to. I couldn't move much because my knee was not cooperating. As the sun was setting, I stopped for the night. I decided to not have a fire this time. I was afraid that other demons may have heard the explosions earlier.

As I lay there inside my improvised tent, freesing my ass, no liquor or a good smoke, and with not much hope for the next day I thought once again about Shamain and wondered where she could be. I tried to keep alert for as long as I could, hoping to not fall into a deep sleep, but I was exhausted. It didn't take long for my head to start jerking.

Chapter 13 -- *Shamain vs. Gaya*

I had the strangest dream that night.

Though everything was happening in front of me, I could not stop it. It wasn't because I couldn't move. I was just frozen in the moment; somewhat aroused.

Gaya was wearing short shorts and ankle--high boots. She was wearing a spaghetti strap top covered by a long sleeve shirt. Her purse was her version of my vest though I don't know what kind of terrors she had stored inside. She had elbow pads, knee pads, wrist guards, and open--finger gloves.

Shamain was wearing tights; high heel boots; a zipped--up fluffed jacket with a furred collar and hoodie. Other than the white fur, everything else was black. Her hair was un-customarily untied.

Gaya and Shamain were standing face to face. Despite them being schoolmates at the academy; this was the first time they made notice of each other, and they were clearly incompatible. I am not exactly sure why.

"Let us through, there is no reason for you to risk injuring your skinny behind today" Gaya said.

"Aw, you called me skinny, thanks. I am sorry sweetie, but if you don't turn around and cease this chase, I am going to split that fat face of yours in half" said Shamain in a snarky tone.

Gaya equipped herself with three swords. They were single edged narrow blades. One of them must have been new; I had never seen it before. The other two made a set -- the winged swords --- it was a symbol of the love between Aiyoo and her. The two swords could combine into a single double edged sword. It made for a bigger, uncomfortable grip, but it could deliver more ethereal energy.

"Who the fuck do you think you are; keep talking to me like that and I'll rip your pussy out.Do you get me sweet heart, or do it need to carve it into you?" Gaya exploded.

Shamain drew a massive sword out her BES. Its guard was ornate with angels. It was a bit difficult to believe that she could wield such a massive sword on her small frame. The sword was glowing, displaying immense power.

"I know who you are; you're that Shamain girl Jackie has talked about." Gaya said "I'd gladly kill you, but since you're his friend I'll give you a chance to change your mind and join us."

"Why would I want to do that? Why would I want to give up this life for your cause? What I want is more power, and only the Emperor can give me that. Soon I will become his wife, and then I will take the crown and rule this empire and I'll rule every little peon just like I control him" Shamain was looking at me when she said her last words.

"I pity you." Gaya said

"Babe, I think it's time for us to dance," Shamain said.

It all happened very fast. Gaya threw one of her winged swords at Shamain as she pulled out her other two. Shamain deflected the projectile at lightning speed though she was using such a massive weapon. As Shamain was blocking, Gaya charged ahead. Shamain readied for a counter. Gaya was close to Shamain's striking distance when she threw a second sword; this one was charged with an explosive spell. The explosion was close to Shamain's face which made her lose her form. Gaya was about to strike, right at that moment the spirit within the sword appeared to control the sword. Gaya changed her direction and headed to her winged sword. She combined them to make the twin sword. Gaya then pulled out her trusty rifle.

Shamain was on her knees, screaming in a painful rage. Gaya was about to shoot, but Shamain's dragon came launching at her. Gaya shot at the dragon at close range and full blast. The dragon fell on the ground, head first.

One particular vulnerability a pet user would have would have been against magic detection because it could show the pet's weak spots; the areas where the ethereal energy was being channeled through. This gave Gaya a slight upper hand since she was a natural detector. Gaya used her winged sword to severe the link between the pet and user. The impact made Shamain lose her focus which made the guardian of the sword vanish.

Gaya was facing Shamain's back. As she was about to strike, Shamain quickly recovered her large sword and swung back with a horizontal strike, launching Gaya away. Shamain landed her hit with the flat side of the sword; the edge on it was sharp enough to cut Gaya's leg. Shamain's right side was burnt from the earlier explosive charge.

Snakes bit Gaya on her shins. They were part of Shamain's pet arsenal. The snakes had an immbolizing spell -- it would immediately cut down on the victim's mobility, and it would slowly paralyze the target.

Gaya started having cold sweats immediately. "Fuck, how did that shit get me?"

"My sweet snakes are hard to detect, they are designed for people like you. They were surrounding you the moment you stepped in to fight me; that is why You mistook their presence as my own aura. I'm sorry honey." Shamain changed her tone "My face, you cunt. I'll make you pay for marring my beautiful face!

Shamain grabbed her sword, and marched recklessly head on. Gaya tried to block the attack, but she was quickly overpowered by the huge sword. Shamain stabbed Gaya on the abdomen; she made the sword go all the way through. But what Shamain failed to note was that Gaya had split the swords. The twin sword's special ability is that while holding one sword, the other one could be controlled remotely. Gaya's sword entered through Shamain's side of her neck and into her chest cavity. They died in that position shortly after while giving each other some very harsh words.

The shock of the moment woke me up. When I opened my eyes, I was confused. I couldn't remember where I was. It took me a moment to realize it was all a dream. I gave out a sigh of relief. It was morning. There was a figure sitting next to me.

Chapter 14 -- *Meeting with Sela*

"Thank me that I found you before anything else. Idiot, you left a trail anyone could follow, and after all those explosions that I heard from very far away; easy target." Sela said.

The sun was behind the silhouette, so I couldn't make up his face at first. My eyes adjusted after a brief moment. Parts of his skin were disfigured, they looked like burn scars. He permanently displayed two more arms instead of one. He had gained some weight, mainly displayed on his belly.

"I checked the place where you found all those demons. They were remnants of a demon gang terrorizing the area; they were the last ones left" said Sela. "In any case, I am impressed. You've really grown up. Nice cycle by the way, I see you've finally got some taste in vehicles."

"Yo, Sela" my voice had dried up. I noted I hadn't said a word in months. I pulled out the comb he gave me. "I came here to find you. Turns out you were the one who found me first."

"Hmm, I came here to see what the explosions were about. I had a feeling it was you for some reason" Sela checked my leg "Well, it seems like you should rest for now. We will move tomorrow. Here, eat this."

I reached for the bag of food sluggishly. My body was really sore from the day before. The bag was full of jerky meat. I proceeded to chew on it slowly.

"Did you find the answer you were seeking for in these lands? How come you just dropped all communication?" I asked as I was eating.

"I had to. As you know, these lands are not regulated by the government, and you can't just go and about as you please. The moment you leave the empire without its permission, you become a wanted target on the reward books. So that's why I had to leave like that. Besides, if the officials found out that I was losing control over myself, they would have harvested me in that instant" Sela said "Which brings me… by now, you must be a deserter as well."

I swallowed by throat. Sela laughed.

"Aeons ago this land was the only area that was not being ruled by the Demon King. This is why this land still belongs to the demon realm. I can hear those demons; they are in hiding under the earth out of fear of the empire, but they are waiting. If you look around, this place hasn't changed much. Demons here can still manifest physically without having to consume a living body. Maybe you noticed that when you saw the band of demons; they were stable" Sela said. "Somehow being here helped calm my own demons; but their voices are much clearer. I almost lost the battle, but in the depth of darkness, the Priestess pulled me out and brought me back. And then she told me that I had yet to fulfill my duty; that I was about to become a hero. But before I could figure out what she was saying I was back on my senses. It sucks that I ended up looking like this though -- ruining my silky skin. Such is life I guess, I can't go back to the Empire, but at least there are some sexy women around these parts. Speaking of which, where is Alon? And what happened to the space expedition you were in? You're back early."

"He was making plans to look for you, but I snuck out of Atlas on my own. I had to come here on my own because I got into some trouble…" I said, hesitant to tell the story since I knew where it was going.

Sela got the story out of my mouth; that's what many hours together would do. He laughed at the whole incident with Gaya; congratulating me on my bold moves and riduculing me for what I decided to do afterwards.

"Fine, go on, have your laugh. But you're right. I wasn't sure what I was gonna do if I found you transformed into a demon," I replied. "I really don't know what I am supposed to do... In case you want to know; the space colony was attacked by zombies. The attack was so large that it brought the entire ship down. According to the information I have, they emerged from the ethereal core in the ship. There have been increased demon activity reports. Just recently I learned that there is a possibility that the whole concept of ethereal energy is not something that should have ever existed. I just wonder if your demon reaction is related to any of these cases."

"I see, some serious shit going down" he said it so casually I could tell he didn't really care. "But what the hell is up with your arm, it looks like you dug your arm into a pile of shit."

"And how would you know that?"

I explained to him my incidents with Shamain and the dream spell I was placed on, and the task the Hero gave me. It took me longer than expected; especially because I had to give him some details on Shamain.

"Hmm... I see where you're coming from. If I gather all the small details, it all points to what you're thinking." Sela said.

He sat there pensive for a moment.

"Yeah, I don't know why this ancient warrior entrusted me with such a task. And I have no clue how I'm supposed to accomplish this task, it's not like I have the gifts you were born." I said

"I'm gonna stop you there," Sela said "Don't ever say that you have no talent. You have the ability to accomplish things. Maybe you can't do the same things I can, but you can do your own things well. Besides, that arm you have now is a testament to your power. If you haven't realized by now, you are the one who is meant to wield that sword."

"I guess… thanks… now that you mention it, what kind of women are around here? I had been riding for two months, and I haven't seen any settlements" I said.

"The area around here is inhabitable. Most people live close to the ocean, west from here." Sela said

"That's weird, I swear I passed that area, but everything was deserted." I said as I brought out my map.

"Let me see this. You fucking idiot! You took a turn here, if you wanted to go there, you are twelve days off! See, you're not on this area, you are here. Thank me that I found you because you were about to enter real demon territory." Sela said.

I just felt like an imbecile. I always had pride with my navigation skills. Sometimes I didn't even like using my trinket. The telecom trinket also had navigational tools.

"Well, the comb you gave me kept pointing at this direction. There was a hair…" I looked at the comb, the hair had disappeared. "Anyways, I thought it was aiming at you."

"So that thing does work" Sela said, "I was around the area hunting for some demons."

"What about the girls/people you said you were with" I asked

"Yeah, can't really bother living too close to people and not do anything. That's not the kind of life I can bother with, at least not for now. I'll take you to the place I'm staying at. Bitches love me over there. You'll probably meet some nice chicks once we get there" Sela said "and now that you're here, we could go and butt fuck some of these demons after that."

"Sounds nice, but what about the Hero of the Sword," I said "I can't just ignore it. I think that is the only way to remove your own curse"

"So you're saying we should go back to the city?" Sela replied, somewhat upset "Is that why you came here?"

"Yes, I can't do this alone," I replied "I kind of need you. If anyone can pull such a task, that's you."

He took a brief moment.

"Then I guess we'll have to come up with a plan. Anyways, just rest for today. We hit the road tomorrow"

It was a calm day, no sign of danger around. We played a game similar to chess -- where I naturally lost -- while we were playing we chatted about our own adventures. Like this one time at a bar when I was still in the space ship; I saw an attractive girl whom I wanted to start talking to. I couldn't even say I was drunk because I only had a few drinks. My well thought out plan was to make her spill her own drink by bumping into her. That way I'd buy her a drink. Well, I got some courage, and I bumped into her, but when I did, somehow I managed to dump my entire drink on her. When that happened, Umaso and Sonja were nowhere to be found.

Or, there was this other incident when I had just got accommodated in colony twenty two. I got to talking with a girl there, she was cute. We hung out a couple times, and then I got her trinket ID number. Problem was, that after that I bombarded her with messages -- did not hear from her again. It was the first time I saw Sela's tears.

Chapter 15 -- *Malak's Camp*

"Didn't you bring a vehicle of some sort?" I asked

"No you idiot, otherwise we would have left yesterday."
Sela replied "I left my cycle to get upgraded back in the
settlement. With all these open roads, you can really hit
some serious speeds."

Sela handed me his *demon buster* -- It was a long club, it
was studded with ethereal crystals at the striking zone. I
used it as a walking stick.

It took three weeks before we started seeing signs of people -
- I took us quite long since I had to keep taking constant
breaks. I could see some areas that were being used for
farming. There were three distinct outposts on the perimeter
of the town. When I asked, Sela told me that people had
been living in the Southern lands for generations. Some of
the people were descendants of those who fought in the *Last
Stance of the Rebels*, the area that is now known as the
barrens near Atlas. I was very intrigued at seeing this place,
and how the Empire was somehow not prosecuting the
people in these lands was a mystery to me. I had never read
of such a place in any of the textbooks. I then realized that I
was something like four days' worth of travelling in my
cycle had I not been attacked.

Being in that town was like going back to a land before the
Mighty Hunter's dynasty. The roads were just trails of dirt.
The houses were made of straw and slabs of wood. Other
than modified busted Leatonian vehicles, ethereal energy
appliances were scarce. However old they were --for those
who could use them-- they were treasures. I would later
learn that the vehicles they possessed were there in case they
had to move to other areas if demons attacked. But thanks to
Sela, they hadn't had the need to move for quite sometime.
It then hit me. If my mission to destroy all ethereal energy
somehow succeeded, people would go back to living like

this; that is until people found other technologies. All of a sudden, ending my own nation's reign didn't seem to be the right thing to do.

Though I missed my cycle, I was glad that I didn't make it into the area on my own. Being a foreigner from the empire would have gotten me in a lot of trouble as soon as I stepped in this territory. I could have gotten shot from any of the outposts before I even had a chance to see them. At least when they saw me with Sela, they were friendly enough with me.

Just like the houses, people were not wearing the latest in fashion. People really lived on the bare minimum. But the thing that struck me the most was that despite all the hardships they had gone through, their faces of the inhabitants were happy just to be there. There were families who although they had a simple style of living they shared love. Seeing them made me want that more than ever.

Sela was the new protector of these people; I wasn't really surprised. From having talks with the people around, I was made known that this particular settlement was much smaller before his arrival. People who got the news of this new hero in the area moved into this group, and they claimed it was time for a new era. What struck me was that despite the big gut he accumulated over the years, girls were still flocking to him. And now he had two extra arms to cop a feel. I could see what he meant when he said I would not be disappointed with the girls.

The only problem I had was that the girls' eyes were focused on him. Well, most girls, there was a particular woman that was not very fond of him. Her hair flowed like silk, smooth and straight, zero split ends.

"I see that you're back and you brought yourself new company" she said.

"Hi, my name is Hadassah. Well, it's easier if you call me Jackie…" I tried to introduce myself

89

She just looked at me with a surly face.

"You seriously need to take a bath. Please go to the bath house. Just try not to use up all the water. Just by your smell you might as well." After she said that, she just waved me off and left.

I was left speechless. It was nowhere near love at first sight, but Malak had just printed her existence in my brain on that moment. She had a commanding presence to her. Despite her hostile welcoming, there was a distinctive kind side that I could see through her face.

It had been a long time since I had taken a bath. It was like washing away all the troubles for at least a moment. I was refreshed. It felt incredible to feel my face free of grime for once. But then I saw myself in the mirror. I wasn't surprised to see my face turned much darker, except for the area around my eyes that was covered by my goggles, which was something I could sport as a rugged look. But the new face I had was just too much. Instead of getting a sexy, macho tan; I got myself a mutt look. All the dirt that was stuck to my face, it seems, worked as a sun block -- giving me white spots. Even pimples would have been better -- which I had a couple of.

Chapter 16 -- *Shooting for New Romance*

It took me a while to adapt to the lifestyle of the people in the settlement. Their culture was also different from that of the Empire; here they believed in mystic magic stuff. They looked at signs and changes in their environment as prophecies. And they had some very strange behaviors, too.

I could really witness how much people respected Sela; he had really changed these people's lives. Whenever people spoke to me; the main topic was him. I didn't mind though.

"So, you came here all the way to find your friend. That's nice of you" Malak said.

I was sitting at an outpost when she came finding me.

"Hi there" I responded, "Yeah, I did come searching for him, supposedly to 'rescue' him, but he doesn't seem to need any rescuing of the sort. What brings you here?"

"I just came to check the view. I was curious to see who the newest member of our family is" her tone was much more courteous than when I first saw her.

"Say, what do you do around here? I mean, you seem to be quite important in this town." I asked.

"Well, I didn't live all my life here, when I was younger my family moved here to escape from the tyranny of the Empire. We who aren't naturals at using ethereal energy are subject to live like slaves. My father is the leader of this tribe. Right now he left for a meeting with...." She stopped "If you're a spy from the empire, I swear."

"Oh no, I promise. I couldn't even qualify for special solo operations." I said

She stared at me with discerning eyes for a moment.

"Ok, I believe you." She continued "The people you see here are people who escaped the oppressive rule of the Empire. Some are also fugitive criminals, but they don't cause trouble for the most part. We don't welcome those who may pose a danger"

"So, what is it with you and Sela? You are rather unfriendly with him. Am I right if I guess that you two had something going on before and it didn't work out? Or maybe you have feelings for him?" I asked

"Hell no" she said it with certainty and proper entonation. "It's nothing like that with him. Sela is the champion of these people. You can see it yourself. But he comes and goes as he pleases, so I can't really trust him. I'm just worried about the day he comes and decides to leave. It's not like there is anything holding him here."

"He's not like that" I replied "he's more responsible than what he seems."

"What about you? What made you come all this way? I know he is your friend, but I got a feeling you didn't come all this way just to see him." She replied.

There was an inquisitive feeling to her tone.

"I didn't really come to take Sela away." I said "Ok, I did come searching for him. But it is more becauseI have some questions that need answering, and he has always been someone who has always known what to do."

"It seems like you hold an important task ahead of you" she said "care to tell? Sorry, I don't mean to intrude, so you don't have to if you don't want to"

Something about Malak made me feel comfortable with her, even at our second meeting. So I went on to tell her the dream spell I was placed under. I took much longer than I expected, again.

I continued, "On my way here, I came to find out; no, I was given the task to somehow correct -- assuming that there is a need for correction -- the path that civilization has been taking. But right now I am not so sure anymore. Being in this town, if all ethereal energy is destroyed, then people would have to live like this"

"Like this?! What do you mean 'like this'" she raised her voice "who the hell do you think you are to be judging the way we live!"

Her anger was not just noticeable on her voice, but on her face as well. Her whole face, especially her cheeks, had turned red. Maybe it was the moment, but I could feel heat coming from her. I was scared.

"It… it's not like that. I didn't mean to say it in a mean spirited way. I am even envious to see how happy people are here" I could feel cold sweat on my brow, "Just that, I mean, I see the people around here, and how they treasure any ethereal artifact. If people were to lose this technology: things like telecom trinkets, and even the medical science, and the power that people gain from it. All the good that we have, it could all be gone."

"So what, listen to your own story. People were given these powers because that is the only way humans can face against the demon realm. Sure, thanks to it people have now been able to move into outer space, but at what price! My people live under the constant threat of demons. We've lost a lot of people over the years, I've lost love, and those I held dear with me. But even then; we who were born outside the mantle of ethereal energy live a life of near persecution. But I rather live here than be living under an empire that all it seeks is power for itself. The empire has become nothing but a system that oppresses the core of being human -- that desire of having a family full of love. I'm sorry if that offends you, but that is how I see it. If I had the ability to change the world -- if I had your power -- I would do it. Sure, people would have to start back from zero, but just look at my people, we may not have all the luxuries you've lived with, but it just is just to show how strong we humans can be. And from everything you've told me, if I were to guess, demons will end up destroying humanity sooner or later."

Her words resonated in my ears like a war cry. After that moment, all my doubts were cleared off, and ever since then I remember being set on my conviction.

"Thanks, I needed that" I said. "I may not be going with Sela, but I will find a way."

"I believe in you. From the little we've met; I find you to be a wholehearted guy. Maybe I am being foolish, but even your story. I want to believe in it, too" she said. Even her soft words had a weight to them "I think Sela should go with you. Though he is the protector, we can live without him. Besides, once you finish your mission, there won't be any demons right?"

We sat there quietly for a moment. I could feel her slightly leaning to me, and my hand was inching towards her hand.

"Anyways, the next shift is about to take your turn. Let's go back to the party." Malak said.

We ended the night eating, drinking, and smoking. It was a blast. I would feel the hangover the next day.

For the next week, Sela was out hanging out with his girls. I was there spending a lot of time around Malak; trying to assist her on whichever activities she had to accomplish that day -- most of the time she would end up scolding me. While she was out on council meetings, she would leave me to babysit her three year old daughter. She was a riot, as in hell. The little girl's father had left them soon after Malak gave birth. The town was planning to make the next move to meet with Malak's father. There was also news that Empire officials were on the trail of their settlement. It had something to do Empire fugitives in the area. My presence raised suspicions on the head council.

I found myself getting closer to Malak, and I could feel her getting attached to me as well. Despite all the troubles she had been through, I could only admire the strength that she had in her.

One night we were drunk atop one of the outposts. She was getting cozy with me.

"This is nice" she said as she leaned her head on my shoulder "hmm, you showered for once."

"Hey! I do usually shower" I said "You want to shoot my cannon?"

"What kind of cannon are you referring to?" She gave me a look

"Umm, my side arm…" I was blushing "it's ok; you can use my cannon as long as I transfer my energy through you. Oh god… I'll charge it low so that it won't be dangerous to anyone or call any attention."

She gave me a flirty look as she grabbed my weapon and leaned her rear to my crotch. She was winding her hips sensually. She was too close to my crotch; I was fighting to not get aroused in order to avoid possible embarassment. I placed my hand on her arm. I had to focus transferring my energy through Malak -- hand cannons required for physical contact from the ethereal user. I had never done such a thing, so I was afraid it wouldn't work and end up making me look like an ass.

"Where should I aim?" she asked.

"That rock down there that is being hit by the torch light." I said while trying not to tremble, "Breathe in and out, slowly. Relax your arms…"

She had a very pleasant smell to her mixed with booze. I had her body tightly pressed against mine, and that made it very difficult for me to focus on anything other than her body. The movement of her back as she was breathing made it all the more difficult to keep cool.

She pulled the trigger. She missed.

"Your hand was shaking" she said as she turned around.

My eyes widened as I was thinking on what to say.

"You're finding me irresistible aren't you?" She grabbed my collar.

Her face was getting closer to mine as I let my attraction to her take over and leaned to her. I swallowed my saliva as our noses touched. And then we kissed. We started slowly. But as she latched on my clothes and tugged my clothes closer to her our kiss intensified. My heart started pounding frantically, and my breathing was starting to get heavy.

In a moment of bravery, my hands found her breasts from under her garments. As I had my hand on her chest, I felt her body shudder in excitement. The softness of her skin was making me lose myself into her.

She started to remove my pants as I pulled off her shirt. Her hands were on my hips, the cold of her hands as she moved to grab my ass made me feel goosebumps running all the way through my back. I exposed her breasts in the air. Her soft breasts bobbed with her movements, and her nipples, those glorious monuments, had my eyes focused on them. Our kissing got more intense, more violent. I reached under her garments, in between her legs. A soft moan hit my ears. I could not stop; I started to frantically take all off her clothes as if I was possessed. Next thing I know, I was naked in front of her, feeling incredibly vulnerable. But her touch reassured me that everything was all right. I was as hard as a rock. Without any effort my penis had found its way inside her. I could feel the moist warmth of her whole. And then I was completely absorbed in the intimacy of her naked body. It was so unexpected, but that night was the greatest thing that ever happened to me.

Ok, I didn't last at all. I was just getting started when my excitement got the better of me. I was embarassed, but her embrace was comforting. We were wrapped up on each other from head to toe. It was the kind of closeness I yearned for all my life. After a moment, I was ready to go again.

The next morning, there was no feeling of awkwardness with each other. After that we would walk around town, and everyone could see it from our eyes that there was something going on between us --she would still yell at me at times though. But we didn't care. We would spend the nights together, and we grew dependant of each other more and more as each day passed by. But then it was time to face the reality that we would be separating eventually and shortly.

We were lying down; her head was resting on my chest. She was a little uncomfortable because my BES was getting in the way. I was drifting into sleep, but not for long.

"I wish this night, these times together never came to end"

"Huh, what do you mean? Is there something going on?"

"Nothing, it's just that I like being next to you too much. And it saddens me to no end to think that we will have to go on our separate ways."

"Forgive me, but the things that you are saying are coming out of nowhere for me... Are you breaking up with me?"

"Not at all, I want to spend as much time as possible with you believe me. But let's face it, at some point you have to go and face that responsibility, that whether you like it or not, you must fulfill it. It is for the betterment of this world. And I can't be too selfish to just keep you for me. Besides, the council is not agreeing with your stay here, not with these empire officials heading our way. The only reason why they allow you to stay is because of Sela, and me. But their patience is wearing thin, once my father comes back they are even thinking of letting Sela go as well. If it was all up to me, I would go with you, but I can't. I can't just leave my daughter behind, and I am sorry that I can't do anything for you as we are."

"No, I understand. I would never be able to put you in such a dangerous situation either. And I know that where I am going, there is a high chance that I may not survive it. And you're right; I can't just run away from this either."

"I am sorry"

"Me too"

"I want us to cherish our moments together for as long as they last"

"Me too… damn it all"

My eyes were teary. I could hear her sobbing quietly in the dark. I embraced her tightly without saying a word. I had a hard time sleeping that night. And it was then when I finally understood.

In between cursing my own luck; I was able to put it all together. Love is not just about all the things that would make two people compatible or how much feeling is involved -- it's impossible when it all comes from one side, but even when two people want to be with each other, sometimes fate can be cruel. Love is heavily dependent on chance, circumstances, and the stage in the person's life. I know my status as a low ranking special officer made a big wall that some girls would build when I tried getting to know them. Maybe if Malak and I had met in a different world, maybe then we could be. But then again, I had to take into account that it was the situation we were in what made her even look at me.

Chance, it felt as if it was all about chance. If Malak had not come visit me at the outpost that first night we would have never talked. Even more so, had I not opened up about my truth, or had I said something stupid, I would not be naked next to her. For that, I was at least glad that chance gave me even this tiny window of time.

But the final piece of the puzzle was rather dissatisfying to me -- mainly because it was not a concise answer. When it comes to Gaya and Shamain -- they just didn't see themselves with me. That was it, simple. Whatever it was, I was just not what they looked for in a guy, no matter how hard I would try to become the man they wanted. I analyzed every piece of minuscule detail on my relationship with Malak, and to no end. There was nothing significantly different between the ways I would get along with any of them -- we all bonded, at least I felt, in a deeper way than the norm. And even when it came to shortcomings, Malak would tell me how I was not her type, and yet she ended up wanting to be with me. I never understood what it was that Malak saw in me.

Addendum -- love is a choice that people make. Given all the circumstances above, a person then chooses whether or not they are going to have feelings for the other. Yes, I have heard many times that people do not choose who they like; that they can't control their feelings. That is a lie. It is Always a choice. Maybe some don't realize it. That is because the choice they make is led by their own emotions or feelings. Let me give you an example of when it may be an almost subconscious act. Two people are getting to know each other. At some point, given every factor is favorable, one of them will think to him or herself, "I like how this feels," or "I am finding this individual to be interesting," or even "I wonder how the sex would be." It is right there the point where that person has the choice to either keep going or to stop.

Love is a choice. And this choice is similar to a person who is about to jump off a cliff. Once the subject has chosen to jump, it is already too late. That person is fucked because the only outcome is that they are going to fall and land somwhere somehow. Maybe he will land on water, or he will smash his brain on a rock. Once someone starts wondering about the what-ifs; things have already started to take motion. Now, I wonder how come I tend to jump by myself so many times.

Chapter 17 -- *Riding off to Battle*

I was glad that after Malak and I had that talk, things didn't really change much. But I couldn't shake off that it would all come to an end soon. And things did come to an end much sooner than I thought.

The alarms sounded throughout the settlement. Everyone was in panic. In the commotion I saw the council elders giving me strange looks. I couldn't find Malak.

The outposts had seen large clouds of smoke over in the horizon. They could make up the profiles of demons the size of a large tree. No one had ever witnessed such a large gathering of demons in one place; whatever their purpose was, it was too close for comfort.

I was helping organize the evacuation according to plan when Sela appeared from the distance. Two very beautiful girls were behind him. I was unfamiliar with one of them. He took a stand. Everyone turned to him yelling their fears at him.

"Everyone calm down! I said, shut the hell up!" Sela yelled, "Look at all of you scatter like rats. You see some demon, and you all get scared. When are you going to stand up and fight? Think for a moment, you can't run from this. If these demons are making their way here, they will pick you out one by one. I will go scout the area and try holding them back while you organize a defensive." He then looked at the elders, "I cannot believe you. The second you see danger you go and blame my friend. He is someone you could count on for anything, and you judge him because it comes easy for you with your bullshit superstition. Fuckers, today you'll be thanking him for saving your asses. Let's go Jackie."

One of the girls brought his cycle out. It was a thing of beauty. It made mine look like a toy. He kissed both his girls before he got on. Right before we set out I saw Malak standing in the crowd. She gave me a smile, but I could see her worry. I smiled back.

"You should say farewell to your girl properly" Sela said.

I jumped out of the cycle, and I hugged her tightly.

"Come on! Give her a kiss you fag!" he shouted.

I was blushing --I was never too comfortable with kissing in public, especially with everyone watching -- but I kissed her anyways, and I could hear Sela cheering on. What a dick.

"You better come back" she said

"I will," I could not feel any more macho than that.

Soon after, we rode off. Sela's cycle was incredibly fast. I could barely hold on the bars. The wind was making my mouth salivate. Good thing I had my goggles on. I then heard him yell through the wind:

"Cool huh? Did you hear how amazing my speech was? I put those punk asses in their place." He said.

"What I am more intrigued is how you got those two girls" I replied

"I actually have four girls," he replied "But I see you with that Malak -- taking over the single mom. You make me proud."

"Dick, why did you tell them I was going save them today?" I changed the topic.

"That smoke is not from coming from demons. There are definitely people involved in there. I saw two LWS units, but there were just too many beasts around, large ones too -- and demons are stronger in these lands. If we don't hurry they are going to lose that battle. Besides, it is time for you to start training."

"Wait a minute, how did you see all of that? Even if you were at an outpost, from what I was told they were on the horizon"

"Demon blood, remember?" He said "I don't know if it's because of this place, but ever since I regained control of the demons, my senses are much better."

"Sela, if you were in my position. Would you still do what I have to do, even if it meant losing all your powers? I am talking about all of them."

"Good question. As long as I can still get with some fine women, and get my dick up, I don't care." He replied, "Can't really help you there. That job is something that has been placed in your shoulders alone. You and only you can do it. But don't worry; when the time comes you'll figure it all out. Until then you can count on me. I'll ride with you to the end."

"Thanks," I replied.

"Hang on tight. I'll show you how fast this baby can go. YEAH" He charged the cycle and unleashed the throttle. I could feel my cheeks turn into flapping rags.

As we were riding, I noticed a couple demons running the same direction we were headed. When I paid closer attention, there weren't just a few. The background was filled by a stampede of demons on both sides.

Sela used his ancillary demon arms to draw two massive hand cannons -- each larger than the one I had. The blast from the cannons was incredibly large -- it was a beam wall that decimated everything on its path. I would say the beams had the same destructive capacity as that of a battleship's.

We cleared a path. I could see what was going on with much more clarity.

"It's time, get to work! Take the front, don't let go of the throttle." Sela said, "And don't fucking scratch the paint! Get low."

As we rode, I could make up a battalion of large demons ahead of us. Most were at least twice my height. Six were as tall as a two story building, and two -- as tall as redwood trees -- were at the flanks of the demon gathering slowly approaching the center while using parts of them as artillery ammo. Behind the smoke clouds I could make up the shape of two customized *Ground Leatonian--War--Suits* and one *Leatonian Civilian Unit.* They were pinned close to a rocky mount. I was surprised they had not yet been overrun. The blast of Sela's cannons made some of the demons turn their attention on us.

I saw two six--shot hand cannons coming from behind my shoulders. Each shot landed on a demon's head.

The increased noise from explosions and the density of the smoke told me that we were close to the LWS fort.

"Keep steady. We're going straight ahead; I'll cut a path open."

Sela then moved in front of me and stood on top of the front wheel fender, pulled out his *demon buster* and an enormous beam came out of the tip. He held this beam spear like a joust. One of the six commanding demons was in front of us; I couldn't make up its exact height, but the damn beast so immense I could not see the face when we got closer. Sela busted a hole through it -- a task that he made look easy; I could never dream to do that. The hit made the demon fall.

I could see a path for us to get through to the mecha units. There was a ring of charred earth on their perimeter. The LWS units were using their shields to block the artillery fire coming from the larger demons. The LCU was housing a number of people who were manning turrets and guns. There were some more officials on the ground. They had used all of their firepower to hold the demons back, but their defenses were wearing thin. The problem to get inside the defensive wall was that there was a group of grunt/infantry demons blocking the way, two hundred paces from the stronghold. Sela took care of that problem.

"Watch it, stop!" Sela yelled. I slammed on the breaks, and swerved sideways. Sela jumped out, but I fell with the cycle instead.

"Damn it! I can't go to war with you. I had a perfect plan, with a brilliant play by me, and you had to go and mess up my ride." Sela said, not minding the situation he just got us into.

"Get up and assist, I am going to take care of that big shit over there." He meant one of the gigantic siege demons. He got on his ride, and rode up to the mountain; while taking care of some demons that had made their way there.

It was deafeningly loud. The area was under heavy gun fire. Demons surrounded every inch of the area; they were slowly starting to close the gap. They relentlessly kept coming at us no matter how many were being shot down. One of the demon leaders had its eyes on me. The nasty smell of burnt rotten meat was the least of my concerns at the moment.

I didn't have time to take the situation all in when I felt a hand on my shoulder. I turned to see, and it was Gaya. She was completely covered in dirt and demon blood.

Seeing her again was a happy surprise.

"Here, I want you to install these around the perimeter, make sure they're one hundred paces away from the center, where Umaso is" She said "Don't worry I'll cover you."

She handed me a bag full of ethereal mines -- similar to my traps. Damn thing was at least half my weight. They were remotely activated. The difference between these and regular explosives is that --as any other ethereal device -- these could channel the user's magic powers into them.

Because of this they could cause a much bigger explosion. Moreover, these were especially effective against demons.

"Why didn't you try doing this earlier?" I yelled as I was struggling to lift the bag "Couldn't you send someone else?"

"Just shut up and hurry" Alon shouted from the LWS's megaphone.

I guess it was some sick welcoming joke. I found out soon after that they did have some installed earlier, but the plan was to have more in order to maximize what would be the final defensive move against this demon siege.

I ran as fast as I could, why did no one else come with me to help install these if it was that important made me think that my own friends wanted me dead. There were fifty of these bombs, each needed to be activated manually, not an easy task. I came close to getting mauled by some demons, but Gaya and company's cover fire did not let me down. Sela's gun saved me from a very close call --he was back from his duel with his personal target. As soon as I was done installing these mines, I was ordered to get in the center. By the time I was done I was so exhausted I could not breathe, I was down on my knees.

Umaso had been gathering all of his ethereal energy into this charge for at least an hour. His effort was so large that his nose was bleeding and he was having a hard time staying conscious. Demons had broken in very close. In one split of a second, a large explosion around the perimeter blew up the vast majority of demons. Leaving others disoriented or wounded.

Sela hit me in the back of the head.

"What the hell are you doing? Let's go finish these fools."

Yes, I was forced to get back up to engage the enemy. Not sure why, Sela was ahead of me and he finished the job on his own.

After the remnants of the demon offensive were neutralized, and the subsequent greetings took part, all the soldiers moved back into Malak's camp.

Umaso, Gaya, Alon, and Sonja were in the group. I would later find out that Malak's father's caravan was with them as well. And to my biggest surprise, Mr. Ham --the Legend from the East, Gaya's favorite teacher -- was among the people in this strange gathering.

Chapter 18 -- *a Fated Reunion*

The bath house was out of order for a day after the new crew came in to refresh themselves. I was put on duty to clean; by everyone's vote and 'request'.

I got quite the scolding from Alon for leaving Atlas without a warning. Umaso and Sonja also ripped my ass as well. Gaya spent the most amount of time cursing at me and my inexistent mother -- the topic of my assault on Gaya was never brought up during this time or ever.

I noticed how Gaya and Umaso looked at each other. I could witness the love between those two just by seeing them there, so happy. I understood then that I could never get in the middle of such a perfect union, and that it was best if I didn't bring up my own selfish interests. I did however; wish that they wouldn't be smooching so much in front of me.

Then I remembered Umaso's penis. I would probably never be able to satisfy Gaya after him...

Being introduced to Malak's father as his daughter's love interest was not something that I was prepared for. There was a raging fire in the man's eyes when he looked at me. His neck seemed to get some sort of whiplash whenever he noticed my presence. He didn't really say a whole lot to me. The throbbing vein in his forehead did all the talking.

A festive mood governed the settlement. Their leader was back, and they had found new allies in -- what I would come to find out -- a new rebel group against the empire. This whole settlement had been planning a final offensive that entailed sneaking in the Atlas tower in order to overthrow the leader. This group had been organizing for quite some time. Their connections extended all over the empire; from what I heard, their people had access inside the tower itself.

Though some members of this movement were among those who lived in privilege; most were people whose families were fated to live nearly as slaves because of their own blood.

It was a meeting that took place around a large bon fire. It was another night of food and liquor. I was already very hung over from the night before when Malak's father made me drink till oblivion. Not sure the things that I may have said or done that night. I am glad I don't remember in order to avoid further embarrassment.

"… It just came natural to me. I just jumped out of my cycle. I must have been really airborne because I think I was at the tip of the demon's helm. I just drew all my eleven cannons [by pulling more ancillary arms, one of his abilities], and let that motherfucker rip." Sela was describing how he destroyed the large demon to his girls. There were now six. They were just mesmerized by his presence as he talked about his heroics. Really, with such a big gut.

"But you should have seen my boy, before he came in the settlement; he fought off a gang of demon zombies, all by himself. Hey, drink up, pussy" Sela handed me more alcohol.

"Really though Jackie, what kind of friend do you take me for. Girl or no girl, sorry babe (to Sonja) I would have come on this journey with you. Never forget we're brothers no matter how much you fuck up" Alon said, for at least the seventh time. He was tomato--faced drunk.

"Thanks guys, but how come all of you ended up here? Why is Mr. Ham here?" I asked, trying to hold my insides.

Gaya spoke, "I ran into Mr. Ham while we were searching for clues on what is really happening with the ethereal ores. Back then, and even now, he had been researching on the link between demons and our powers. He believed that our incident at the barrens was a key event to the truth. And that event leads to you somehow. He is here to see why"

"While you were gone; we did a lot of work together trying to get all the pieces together. You decided to give yourself a sweet vacation while not only we were wondering where you were, but I had to fill up all of Gaya's paperwork" Umaso said, with a smile "ever since I met you I knew that there was something different about you. I guess it is time for you to know that you were intentionally assigned to me by some heads in the Empire. One of my secondary objectives was to always watch over you; back then, I didn't know what the reason was. I hope that you don't take that offensively. You are one of my best friends now. And had it not been for you, I would have never met Gaya again. And don't worry about having run off. Sure, we created some enemies along the way, but this whole thing also opened our eyes about some things about the Empire that I do not like."

"Before we got attacked by those demons, we were being tailed by Empire officials. They seemed to be looking for you too." Gaya said "When we finally forced them to retreat, they used a device to summon all those demons. It's quite terrifying to think that the Empire now wants to use demons as pets now."

It felt awkward to hear some of the things Umaso was saying. I had a feeling he knew about what happened between Gaya and I. Gaya, on the other hand was somewhat distant from me at this point; meaning that there was absolutely no physical contact with her -- as in friendly hugs; I didn't expect anything else. And she started reprimending my comments and jokes whenever they were of the sexual nature.

The conversation led for me to tell them about the spell dream I had about the Hero of the Sword. Somehow I avoided mentioning Shamain.

After I was done, there was a brief moment of silence. Except Sela, who was mocking Alon's face and laughing to his heart's contempt. Everyone else was pensive.

"So it all makes sense now. Who would have known you've held the key all along," Mr. Ham laughed while chugging on some liquor. He was pretty drunk too.

"Before I forget, I found you this," Sonja handed me my own trinket back "I found it as we were searching for you. Yes, that is how we found out where you decided to sneak into. A 'thank you, beautiful princess' would be nice"

"Thanks, but you're not a princess, and definitely not beautiful," as I said that, I looked at Alon, luckily he was too drunk to hear me. It was really difficult getting used to these new couples.

The next day we went over the plans to get back into the capital city, and subsequently sneak back into Atlas tower. The mission: steal the Demon King artifact.

The idea of giving up on the powers sent by heaven hit some people hard. Among my friends, Alon seemed to be bothered the most. Perhaps it was the fact that he knew that his beloved mechas depended on ethereal energy. When I approached him, he would tell me with a smile not to fail my mission. Mr. Ham however, kept the argument that destroying the Demon King artifact was too premature of an idea, that maybe we should use the artifact itself to seek other alternatives. Removing the Demon King artifact should halt some of the effectiveness of Atlas' defenses -- though there were no exact numbers. Majority agreed.

Everybody had their own roles in this guerilla offensive. This plan took an entire generation of people to develop, and its final execution was soon to take place. And much of its success depended on my own performance. My mission objectives: retrieve the Hero Sword; reach the Emperor's room and use the sword to assist in dethroning the Imperial head if necessary. No pressure.

Mr. Ham came to a conclusion after looking into my arm that deep inside me; ever since I was born; my whole purpose was to be the bearer of the sword. With that, I had the ability to be able to sense where the sword is located at any point in time -- in more accurate terms; I could sense the spirit of the Hero of the Sword. That my left arm was the way it was because that person stole part of that power.

Mr. Ham then installed a tracking device in my trinket. This add-on device was something he used to find rare artifacts that had a linking to the supernatural: ethereal energy, demons, wraiths, etc. Since the device was now assimilated to me, according to Ham's calculations, it would lead me to find the sword, and with that, to Shamain.

When I turned on Ham's device, I immediately knew where the sword was. Unlike Sela's comb, this new compass was accurate. I was shocked when I learned that it guided me to Atlas tower itself; I didn't understand why would the sword be in there. I could really feel the sword and the person holding it. It was downright bizarre.

After that night, the whole camp started making preparations. Malak's father spent much of his time analyzing the demon summoning artifact -- he used to be one of the Empire's top scientists. From what Malak had told me, when she was still living in the empire, her father had been developing the technology that would allow non-- gifted people to use ethereal tools. The lack of interest by heads of the Empire caused the project to be shut down.

I didn't get much time to spend with Malak, and every time we were together there was a rather uncomfortable feeling in the air --she was more uneasy than me with the situation. Other than learning the details of my mission, I spent most of the time running errands for whatever people demanded. Other than that, there wasn't much of anything else going on during downtime. One thing that really caught my attention though was Sela and Umaso's sparring session.

That fight lasted for hours. One morning, Sela's blood had the urge to fight. Umaso accepted the challenge. The rules were: no use of ethereal weapons, either melee or ranged; Umaso could not use his energy blasts; and Sela had to limit his demon ability to his two auxiliary arms. Sticks and stones were replaced as their weapons instead.

Even with such limitations, the two of them managed to level the landscape. Umaso got an early lead in points -- a scored was awarded every time it could mean certain death in a real fight scenario. Sela eventually caught up. The fight was stopped because the sun had set, dinner was ready, and both men started moving sluggishly. The score ended at ninety one points to Sela and ninety two points to Umaso, giving him the lead.

Their injuries called for some recovery time; delaying the whole operation for three days. After that they were not allowed to spar again.

The time to move into action came at last. This marked the point when I had to say goodbye to Malak. She was moving with her camp to a safe location overseas. As a contingency, their plan was to move to remote places in the Empire as pirates to gather as much resources in order to continue the fight. After the demon stampede, no one felt safe being in the south lands. Mr. Ham was to join them. I didn't like the way he was looking at Malak though.

Sela, Alon, Sonja, Umaso, Gaya, and I were the squadron in charge of infiltrating inside Atlas city, where we would rally with other supporters of the cause. Two members from Malak's camp came with us to get us through with the rebels.

Malak was bawling during our final goodbye.

"Promise me that you will come back. Tell me that you love me."

I promised her, but when I told her that I loved her, it did not feel very pleasant. All that time I was sure of my feelings for her, but as much as I wanted to I couldn't give her my whole heart. A part of me was focused on the Hero sword and Shamain.   When I realized how I really was, I felt like the biggest coward.

As much as I wanted to go back to her after everything was finished; I never got the chance. That was the last time I ever saw her. My eyes were focused elsewhere.

Chapter 19 -- *Whispers of Lust*

I could feel how she loved her new possession. The way she was on the edge of obsession with him was the way that I yearned for her to feel about me. I could feel how easy I was getting filled with nasty jealousy. More than anger, I felt disgust.

'Come out babe, I want to see you.' I heard her whisper to the sword.

'Don't overexert your energy, you'll exhaust yourself. I don't want you getting sick,' the sword replied.

'I don't care. I don't want to be alone right now.'

'We share the same pain of what it feels like to be truly alone. For all I can remember, I have been in this prison of no purpose. And you have been the guiding lighthouse in my existence. And since, I want to know how it feels like to be laying with you.'

'And I want to claw my nails in your muscles.'

'And I want to take your pain away.'

'Do you feel this? I want you inside me. I want you thrusting yourself against me. Make me moan; make me grunt as you make me yours. I want to lay helpless as you cover me in the mantle of your fury. Can you feel my craving, the heat between my legs? It is all for you'

Her breathing was getting heavy, irregular, as her heartbeats were getting louder as they got faster.

'Why are you doing this? To what purpose am I in here if I am to be trapped here if I cannot flay your garments off?' The sword let out a burst of rage.

'You are here for me'

She embraced the sword as it cut her skin.

'I feel lonely' she said as her voice saddened

'You must have a friend somewhere other than me.'

'No.'

The sword went quiet as I heard her cry.

Chapter 20 -- *the Rebel Offensive*

It was not my intention to be listening to that conversation. It hurt. After I heard all of that, I shut down the device Ham installed. I only turned it on periodically to find out where the sword was.

'No' such a simple word, and yet it could strike someone like a dagger. The way she said that so easily and without second thought was what hurt me the most. I offered her all of my services, she refuses, and then now she doesn't even acknowledge me.

Maybe it was too selfish for me to think that way. I never knew what troubles she was going through, and I was not in the position to be of any help given her circumstances. It could be that, but in reality I knew and I felt somewhat responsible. She knew that I didn't just see her as just a friend -- spell or no spell. And until the very last moment I saw her, I could not accept the fact that I was not the guy for her. My foolish endeavor of keep trying is what caused her to shut me down the way she did.

Everyone in the squadron was tense; we were all considered deserters from the Empire. If anything went wrong, we would all be dead.

'Great, this is by far the stupidest idea I've partaken in. Hey, someone pass me some more of that booze!' Alon yelled on the radio from his LWS

'Honey, please stop drinking' Sonja replied from inside her suit.

'Hey, know your own damn place!'

'Who the hell do you think you are; don't you dare talk to me like that. You're out of your damn mind if you think I will let you treat me like this...'

117

'No! Hey! No! You are disrespecting my fucking rights! I want my drink now!'

On and on, those two were arguing while everyone could hear them from the radio channel. The rest of us were inside the LCU, trying to ignore it. That was the third time in two days.

"Are you ok?" Gaya asked me.

"Yes"

"I know you're lying. Tell me!" Gaya insisted "is it the mission, your girlfriend… or, is it me?"

"No, actually, it is Shamain"

"Oh, I think I remember you telling me about her…"

"That incident in the barrens, when she came to the rescue, the sword she took with her was that same Hero Sword. I never told you that. Now she is inside the tower as my enemy. That means I must fight her in order to get a hold of that sword."

"Don't worry. She is your friend, so I'm sure she will come around. Just try not to think about it."

'Jack! Come here, pilot the suit. I'm going to steam up Sonja's cockpit' Alon messaged me on the trinket.

'Dude, no need to give me all that info; make sure you turn off the radio' How disgusting.

At the border between the empire and the southern lands; we reached at the rebellion meeting point. The connections went through smoothly, but there was tension in the air. I could feel people giving me heavy looks when they found out who I was and what role I was about to play. Some people got aggressive towards me. Sela stepped in, when they learned who he was, they withdrew.

Friction aside, final preparations took place without a hitch. The rebels trusted Sela -- a half breed was now looked up as the leader.

The operation involved three stages. Everything was already set in motion. I looked at the plans, and the amount of people involved in this offensive was shocking. Somehow the rebellion had in their possession eight squadrons of three LWS units. Some were ancient models, but even so; the age of these war suits was proof to the generations this rebellion had been preparing itself for.

The first stage involved all the armed rebel forces to make their presence be known to the Empire's capital. Ready to fight, their goal was to stand their siege at the East side of Atlas. This was in hopes to have the city's defenses be aimed at them.

With an armed force present. The city would then raise its walls against the oncoming army. I had never seen these walls being raised, but I had heard the legends. These walls were as tall as a mountain range, and just as thick. Nothing would be able to penetrate them.

When Atlas would rise its walls; that is when stage two --the true offensive-- would commence. The walls took less than an hour to stand at its zenith. This was enough time for a rather small armed force to sneak in. With all the attention aimed towards the east; a squadron composed of Sela, Umaso, Gaya, Sonja, two other rebels, and myself would infiltrate through the southwest entrance --just north of the barrens. The idea was that the barrens presented the worst area for an offensive against Atlas since the terrain would completely favor the city's defenses; with this in mind, the Empire's officials would place that area as low priority.

The key squadron was chosen based on proficiency. Since we all knew each other and we had some experience working alongside, my group was the better qualified. A small group of soldiers required that all of the members were capable on their own field. Umaso would be at the helm;

Sela was the needed powerhouse, he would be at the front in his cycle; Alon and Sonja would be piloting the LWS assisting Sela with firepower; the rest of the squadron would then infiltrate the tower through the back service entry; Alon and Sonja were to follow by foot after securing the perimeter. We would rely on the two rebels to guide us through to the Imperial room where the Demon King artifact was believed to be. We had to believe that since no attack had ever even got close to the tower, there wouldn't be many guards.

The last stage of the offensive was added at the last minute as a precautionary move. It was an all--in move that carried a lot of controversy, and put a lot of weight on my shoulders. Malak's father had studied the demon summoning emitters. He even managed to create a dozen cloned systems that had twice the power of the original. The rest of the manufacturing would be finished at the meeting point. Once finished, these would be placed hidden in front of the rebel front. As a last hope move, these would be activated.

This last stage could pose great danger against everyone involved. If this whole plan failed; if I didn't fulfill my mission on time, many innocents would lose their lives. The thought crossed my mind a number of times. What if we did get to the Demon King Stone, and all our efforts accomplished was end the ability for humans to use magic. Without ethereal powers humanity would go back to hiding from demons at best. But even then the risk of using these bombs outweighed everything else. The rebellion would not get another chance like this. And taking into account the incidents such as Colony twenty two's, humanity could be doomed either way. Everyone just hoped that these emitters would never have to be used.

Umaso was handed one of the demon emitters as a contingency.

'This is not good. There shouldn't be so many guards on this side. Everyone, embrace yourselves. We are fighting these fools!'

Sela shouted on the radio as we were being fired by the flying drones above us.

We were in the middle of the city. We had passed the wall line. Without any chance of retreating, our only move was to charge forward towards the middle of the city. The two LWS took out some of the drones, but there were more approaching.

'Fuck! What the hell is going on in the front line! I'll cover the rear. Sonja, take care of the units coming at three o' clock!' Alon yelled *'I think we are separating here. Good luck. Jack, if you fuck this up...'*

'Will do' Umaso replied *'Sela, clear the path for us. Destroy any tower that you see'*

'Already on my way fool'

'When we're done I want to race you'

The rest of us were inside a civilian shuttle. It was modified for the mission with defensive weapons. Originally designed for space exploration; this rare vehicle was capable of both land and air movement. We hit the sky.

I could see on the horizon, there was a large battle taking place east. Below us I could see the defensive turrets being taken down by Sela's cannons. Without any threat, I don't think Atlas had updated any of its armaments since the old age.

We made it inside the tower like planned, from the back service entrance.

One of the rebels hacked into the system and closed the gate behind us. As we opened the door to the main lobby on the first floor, we were greeted by an entire company of eighty elite Empire soldiers.

Umaso got attacked from behind by one of the rebel members that were with us. Umaso took him out with a single strike.

"I see, so that is how they found us out. They had spies -- how amateur of us," Umaso grinned "Gaya, take Jack and our other friend -- go ahead without us, we'll catch up."

"Aiyoo, make sure you do that," Gaya replied.

Umaso took out the demon-emitter, and he threw it.

"I just can't bring myself to fight my own comrades without the proper dignity of a warrior."

"I am with you, but in that case; let me even out the numbers."

Sela then sprouted eighty demon clones from behind him. They looked like humans, but they didn't seem to have skin. I noticed each one of them had a long dick. Sela was armed with twenty ancillary arms this time. The battle started.

"You piece of shit, what are you waiting for, get moving!" Sela yelled at me.

Gaya then pulled me as we ran and went into the side door. Since the elevators were blocked, this route would go through the stairs. The place was a massive labyrinth of back paths, even with a map in my trinket, I was still lost. I was glad that our teammate had studied the area in depth. The echo of our footsteps was the only thing I could hear. The silence of our surroundings was frightening in a sense. The world outside was loud; waiting for the outcome of our actions.

"I am so sorry. I didn't know he was a spy. Fuck, I even had drinks with him… I told him everything about my family, too." the rebel soldier cried as we were running.

"It's ok," Gaya replied "he was a trained to do his job well. No one knew."

"We're close. The entrance to the imperial house is behind this hall. The throne room should be on the far side of the first floor,"

The three of us entered the area. Despite us being inside the tower, the place felt more like cavern. The smooth surface of the tower walls was now replaced by rocks. We proceeded cautiously.

The rebel soldier was in the front. I was on the middle while Gaya covered our rear. As we turned passed a stalagmite; in one swift move, the scout in the front got decapitated right in front of me.

"Come out to play, babe."

There was a single guard standing between us and the gates of the Imperial house. She was standing on a platform that led to a precipice on the sides. Shamain's eyes were as bright as two white lamps in the darkness.

Gaya stepped three paces in front of me.

"Let us through, there is no reason for you to risk injuring your skinny behind today"

This was déjà vu. I was about to witness two of the people that I cared for the most die in an instant. I was frozen. I had to do something, but I didn't know what. I thought of the scenario, and if I did something, one of them would end up dying.

"Aw, you called me skinny, thanks. I am sorry sweetie, but if you don't turn around and cease this chase, I am going to split that fat face of yours in half"

Their weapons were ready.

"Who the fuck do you think you are; keep talking to me like that and I'll rip your pussy out.Do you get me sweet heart, or do it need to carve it into you?"

I drew out my gun. I charged it to a non--lethal level. I aimed at the back of Gaya's neck. This time I didn't miss. Gaya was knocked out -- maybe it wasn't the smartest move, but I was afraid she would have not hesitated in killing Shamain. Shamain took this opportunity to strike her opponent.

I pushed Gaya aside, ready to take the hit in her stead. I raised my left arm to block the attack. It was as if my left arm had taken a life of its own. My palm was the first to receive Shamain's thrust attack. The sword penetrated through the middle of my arm, up to my shoulder. My arm was sliced in two. The shocking pain was immediate, but I stood there holding on to the blade with my entire arm, not letting go. Shamain was fighting to take the sword out. At this point, I was connected with the sword and the spirit inside.

"Ah! Please stop! It really hurts!" I yelled "Please"

Shamain's eyes were clouded in tears, dimming down the brightness of her eyes.

"Fuck you!" She cried "let go! I'm going to drain your life away! You don't deserve to have your own powers. You annoying useless piece of shit, just get your ugly face out of my sight"

"Fine, I will. But you have no choice but to listen to me first. I understand why you're here. You were born with special powers, and those in charge of taking care of you did not see you as more than that ability of yours. You were secluded from the world; unlike me you were never able to make friends because you were kept in the dark. The power that you hold made you destined to the spirit within this sword that you hold so dearly. And then you tracked me down. You knew about my own self long before I did. And somewhere along the road, you saw something like a friend in me. Shamain, you know why I am here. And the reason why you can't let me through is because you are afraid to lose him. But what is the point of living that way? They say

Heaven's Stone can grant a wish at the cost of a life. I will make your wish mine. Please, just this one time take that risk with me. I promise you as a friend. I beg you, let go. I'm sorry if I make little sense, but I am losing a lot of blood right now."

Her grip softened. She fell on her knees, and she didn't move.

"I love you," she said in a soft voice.

"As a friend, I know. I love you, too"

About my speech to Shamain, I was wrong. Her truth was different. Yes, she was treated like an animal when growing up. Scientists made experiments on her to enhance her abilities. She was not alone though, she had many friends who had become her family. None of them survived the rough experiments. It was then when in her loneliness she could feel the call of the spirit within the sword. It was then when the Emperor found out what she could do. She was the key to finding the sword that he was looking for ages. That sword was the last instrument that could pierce the demon artifact. And so she found it.

It was not until Colony twenty two when she found out that I had something to do with the treasure. It was by order of the emperor not to kill me -- yes, she would have terminated me then. He didn't want the spirit within the sword to fully awaken. He never expected for me to survive though, nor did she. When I was escaping Atlas, what she felt was closer to pity rather than kinship. I happened to remind her of one of her childhood siblings whom she regarded as a little brother, this weakling she would always look after -- funny, because I am actually older than her.

She could sense me just the way she could sense the sword. She knew I was close to the tower, that is why she was there waiting for me. She did intent to kill me, slowly. But she changed her mind when I mentioned the one thing she knew I was right on. Living a life loving someone she could not touch was something she could not bear any longer. That is why she decided to take that risk with me. And yes, when she said she loved me; that was true as well. That is a very strange way to love someone… I found out this truth at the very last moment of my time in this world.

I pulled out of the sword from of my arm as I left Shamain behind. My arm started healing immediately as I felt gaining strength from the sword. As much as I wanted to sit with her; there was nothing I could do. That and my friends were in danger of dying if I didn't hurry up. I got my left arm back after all this time. I felt incredibly strong. Nothing would stop me.

'Oh, my angel, we meet again. I guess this time we are switching roles.'

Chapter 21 -- *the Hero Rises*

*'First of all, I already have my own angel. The problem is
that you decided to go and fall for her. Fine, I fell in love
with your wife, but that is still no excuse. I cannot believe
the nerve of you, you make me responsible for all of
humanity, and then you go and take my angel away.'*

*'You know I can read your mind right? From what I can see
here, she isn't particularly your one and only... Anyways, I
don't think that is the most important thing to be talking
about right now. I am in your debt once again; thanks to
you I have fully regained my spirit and my memories back. I
can sense him now; my brother is behind that door'*

I opened the door, there he was. He looked just like I
remembered him in my brief time travel. The Mighty
Hunter was sitting down on the throne, on the opposite side
of the hall. He actually looked younger than in my dream.

"So she didn't kill you. Cute story the idea that Heaven's
Stone can grant a wish; that fairy tale is something I made
up to entertain children -- It ws quite interesting to see how
the version of the story has changed over the course of
generations. She is such a nuisance. I let her run about as
she pleased, and look at the disappointment. I should have
disposed of her a long time ago."

"Watch your mouth! She is not your toy" I growled through
my teeth.

"Hmm, but it seems like you are hers. Don't forget who
you're talking to, boy," the Emperor's face turned a
frightening look. My fist was clinching on the sword.
"Well, I am glad that you're here. Never did it occur to me
that you were the key that would bring my own brother back
after all these years. My boy, you have done me a great
favor. Now that I have all of the celestial weapons in my
possession, I will complete the master plan. I can see the

curiosity in your eyes. Don't worry, I will tell you. I have all the time in the world. Oh, I recall now, you are one of the survivors from colony twenty two. Yes, you were assigned to Project 86276, Umaso -- another child that decided to take his hand against me, pity. Ok, I guess I am bored, so I will tell you. That colony was my new laboratory. Humans are weak; always crying when there is no food on their plate; always defenseless like lambs to the slaughter. Creating soldiers like that little girlfriend of yours (Shamain) causes too much waste. But then there are those like your friend, the child of the Priestess. Yes, creatures like him are easier to manufacture. If we humans took the essence of demons themselves, we could come closer to become gods. Sadly, that whole experiment failed, so I must apologize. Right now you could have been one among those worthy of walking the earth. Silence! What I will do now, is reunite with my brother. I will guide his lost soul to become one with me. His sword is the last piece I need to forge a new power to unify all the creatures of the earth; humans and demons will become one, and I will be the guide to take on heaven itself!"

"I don't understand what would all of that accomplish, but regardess, I won't let you. I won't let you take our humanity away. I hear your words, and they are the sounds of a child consumed in the madness of his own power. How can you hope to take on God, he who is the one who granted his children, us people, with the blessing of this power you hold? You are seriously dreaming if you think you can kill a tree with its own seed."

"Well, that seed has grown."

The Mighty Hunter raised his finger and pointed it at me.

A heavy pressure shot me to the far side of the hall. My entire body was filled with cuts. The new strength that I had found earlier was gone.

"Hmm, you survived" I heard the Hunter from a distance.

'That was close,' the Hero spoke

'What are you talking about? I never thought the emperor could be this powerful. I can't even move my hands. I think this is it. I have failed.'

'We should have been turned to dust, but yet you're still in one piece. So don't despair. Lend me your body, you have done enough by yourself, together we will our honor by destroying this curse he calls power. That man standing in front of us is no longer my brother.'

I felt a new surge of power flow through my body. The bleeding stopped. The hero stood back up. He marched forward, determined.

"You are not the brother whom I once stood side by side in countless of battles. Who are you?"

The emperor burst in laughter.

"Brother, so you've come out. After all these years, boy, I am glad to see you're still just as energetic. I am still your older brother, punk. I just so happen to have found the source of a new power. That same power has granted me with immortality."

"There is something else inside of you."

"It is all me. After you left, I infused the Demon King itself into my being. Oh, you would not believe how good it feels to be this strong."

"Ever since that day, everything that you have set to do has been on the wrong path. I am trying to reason with you. If you do not stop, demons will once and forever take over. You cannot control a power that was never yours. For these past one thousand of years I have felt the demon world gaining strength. They will come back to this earth with an army that not even you with all this power could ever stop. I will ask you one more time, please stop. I see, so then I will have to help you see the light!"

The Hero charged ahead. The emperor raised his palm, blasting my body with even more pressure than before. With his sword in front, the Hero kept his own ground and stabbed the emperor through his heart. The sword did not go through. The hero then kept on chopping at the emperor, but his skin would not be cut. No matter how much energy I put on the sword, I could not do any damage. I ran out of energy. I feel on my knees. I was exhausted to the point I could not breathe. The hero still held on to the sword.

"If you had joined me, you would have never had to take a thousand year journey, only to end up dying for nothing. I must compliment you, nobody has ever come this far."

"Close, so close." I said, with a smile. "You win. I give up. I just hope that you do not let down the people that you rule with this new drive."

The Mighty Hunter drew out his spear.

"Good. Now brother, let me help you fulfill your own destiny!"

The emperor swung his spear at my chest, but an incendiary blast stopped his path. I turned my head to see who shot.

"I can't believe you shot me you jerk!" Gaya was holding out her rifle cannon -- customized for more powerful long distance accurate shots -- smoke was coming out the tip of the barrel.

Sela and Umaso were standing to her sides. Shamain was stading behind as well.

"I had expected more of a challenge from the so called elite imperial guards, your royal royal assness." Sela grinned through his teeth.

"Ha. Ha. Ha. Is that the best line you could come up with?" the Mighty Hunter "Stupid little pawn, since you're here I will show you how daddy likes to spank his children. And you Shamain, rebellious child, I am so disappointed in you."

"We're here to stop you from leading humanity into the chaos of being slaves to demonkind! Prepare yourself!" Umaso declared.

"What is this feeling... my hands, they are shaking... is this fear? Ha! Nah, it's just a hangover; or maybe it's all the magic aphrodisiacs I took just a moment ago. After a thousand years, a man needs help even when he is about to rape some little children."

"Alright Jack, we'll hold him back. Go and find that god damn artifact!" Sela yelled "Hurry the fuck up! Get to work!"

Bastard didn't even give me a moment to react, and he was already cursing at me.

The emperor was trying to finish me off, but Shamain had his wrists chained to her chest -- it was a very strong control spell.

"Ah well, it has been a while since I had a sparring session, this should be fun. Come at me with everything you have!"

The emperor stepped on my head and lunged towards my friends. I gathered the energy to get up and scurry to find the artifact.

'Partner, wait. The jewel is not hidden inside any of the rooms here. Concentrate, you can sense it as well can't you. The Demon King artifact is hidden within my brother. Right now is not the time to leave your own brethren behind. Only by being together we'll have the best chances of stopping my old brother.'

'Ok then, my angel, let's do this!'

'YEAH! I like your spirit. Let our will burn with the flames of passion! Let's Go!

The sword got covered in an intense beam of white, and it increased in size. I could feel its sharpness in the air.

I turned around, and I saw the emperor's back was towards me. I sprinted to catch up with him, but he was faster than a demon.

The emperor let out a burst of pressure out of his mouth targeted at Shamain. She was knocked back; the rest of the group was immobilized for a split second. In a single jump, he kicked Umaso on his chin, knocking him down. He followed it up with a double kick that landed on Gaya and Sela. The hunter had his spear aimed at Shamain.

'I can't let that happen!'

I drew my short sword, and I charged it with as much ethereal energy it could hold -- normally that task would take a lot out of me, but it was either my desire to protect those that I held dear or the borrowed spirit force from the Hero of the Sword that it helped me match the emperor's speed.

I could see a clear path. I was possesed with a focus on my target that was stronger than even my battle against the zombie gang. I threw my sword at the emperor with everything I had. I could feel my skin on the verge of ripping apart from the force. My sword flew as fast as a bullet. It stuck on the Emperor with enough force to send him flying up towards the wall, away from Shamain.

"The jewel is inside the emperor!" I yelled

"If he wants to reach heaven so badly, then let's help him by shoving a rocket up his ass!" Sela yelled.

"You talk too much, but let's make sure he feels this one!" Umaso said "Gaya, ready?"

"Lock and loaded. Shamain, let's go!"

"Count me in." Shamain replied.

… I didn't get included in their team rally.

132

Sela drew out twenty cannons -- he stole twelve cannons
from the imperial guards. Gaya overcharged her rifle.
Shamain armed herself with a very small hand cannon from
inside her thigh -- it was so small only the tip of the cannon
was noticeable when she gripped on to her weapon. Umaso
was holding two throwing knives, charged. I held onto
Sela's present, making sure I didn't miss while readying my
short sword to explode. We aimed up. On signal, we pulled
the trigger. We let the sky brigthen in a destructive flash --
it left a hole in the house's ceiling.

A lump of mass fell from the ceiling, covered in fire and
smoke. The Mighty Hunter was still standing, unscathed.
His smile could be seen past the smoke, and the flash in his
eyes showed he was just getting started.

Sela pulled two more clones. The emperor threw the spear
at Sela. He did not have time to react. The spear pierced
through Sela's clones and into his shoulder, and Sela was
thrown all the way to a wall where he was nailed to.

I rushed with my sword.

The hunter was now even faster. In the time it took to get in
range to attack the emperor he kicked Umaso, sending him
off flying. He then back handed Shamain to the ground.
Gaya tried to retaliate with her swords. The emperor blocked
her attack with an equipped shield, swung his axe at her.
Gaya barely dodged the strike from it being fatal, but she got
injured. A tackle from his shield sent her off flying towards
Umaso's direction. The emperor sensed my attack coming
from his back. He grabbed Shamain by the head and threw
her at me.

I had to let my sword down to catch Shamain. I saw the
emperor's eyes aimed at me; I could feel his breath. His
axe was about to chop my head when countless of Sela's
clones rushed at the emperor. Hungry demons were
viciously stabbing the emperor. Sela pulled the spear from
out of his shoulder. His wound was bleeding profusely.

Shamain had a tight grip on my shoulders. Her pale face showed the terror in her.

"We can't… we can't stop him. He's just too powerful. Jack, we need to get out of here."

"Shamain, I promised you. No matter what it takes, even if my bones shatter; I will not let this motherfucker touch you again. Put your faith in me and I'll get us through this one. Get up! You can't just keep living on like this; you were the one who told me that you'd rather die than live a life tied down as a slave… if we all lose now we are all dead. Together we can bring this bastard down. Come, take my hand, face that fear head on because without you right now I'd shit myself."

She didn't say anything. Her hands were still shaking. I was hoping to get a smile out of her with my last line, but I guess the joke had run thin by then.

The emperor blew away all of Sela's minions with an area blast. Sela charged forward, all out. Four cannons were being held by his ancillary arms. Each cannon was charged over their limits, smoke was coming out of the cracks in the cannons. The crystals in Sela's demon buster club were shining with his rage. Sela's wound was pouring blood agressively.

Sela pulled the triggers. The Hunter raised his shields, but still got knocked back. The impact of the ethereal shells caused the emperor to leave an opening. Sela swung his club. The thunderous sound of the hit hurt my eardrums. The emperor's robe came off, as he was holding the demon buster under his armpit.

The Mighty Hunter cast--equipped a full armor on his body. The plates on this intricately adorned armor glistening were blinding. The hunter pulled out a war hammer. With one swing, he broke Sela's club. The emperor then opened up a massive cannon from his chest. Sela brought out four more cannons. At zero range, they blasted away.

Sela tried using clones to get away from the epicenter, but the emperor got a hold of his arms; breaking them. After the blast cleared, Sela was lying on the floor. The emperor stood. He then raised his hammer, ready to crush Sela.

Gaya shot at the emperor, but it did not have any effect. The emperor was still about to finish off my friend.

I rushed forward and swung the sword the Emperor's head. He dodged, and swung the hammer at me. I used the sword as a shield. The force from the hit made me lose sense of self briefly at the moment of impact.

Umaso rushed forward opposite my side with a long sword and hit the Emperor's wrist; making him drop his hammer. While the emperor was busy battling Umaso; Gaya used her winged swords' ability to plunge the sword to plunge in the emperor's foot which made him flinch. Umaso then used his abilities to land a flurry of energy blasts coming at every direction.

Umaso had six blades inside his BES. Two of them short knives -- he already threw them on the first attack. He had two standard swords. He also had the long sword, his preferred weapon. His most powerful sword was a massive blade, I had never seen him use it because he claimed it drained his energy; it was just that powerful considering his own abilities.

He casted out all four of his swords; each one was coated with his energy to maximize on sharpness. In one quick move, he stabbed the emperor with his standard swords. His long sword pierced the back of the emperor through his collar. Umaso then brought out his ultimate sword to slash the Emperor in half.

The emperor quickly cast-equiped another set of armor with a sword made of flames. The armor and sword were black. The emperor used the sword to deflect Umaso's finishing attack. He then drove the sword into Umaso's leg. Another pressure blast, he sent Umaso flying across the room. The emperor then picked out each of the swords in him as if they were splints.

Sela grabbed the emperor's hammer with his teeth and swung at the emperor's chest. The hunter met his boot with Sela's face.

Shamain who was next to me cast magic lines onto the emperor.

"I will disarm his armament. Make it count" she said softly with a determined tone.

Shamain's magic lines made the emperor's armor fall to the ground, leaving him completely naked. Another spell shut down the Emperor's BES -- it was latched right on his belt line.

I plunged forward with the sword, aimed at the hunter's chest.

The emperor let out another pressure blast. Though I tried to fight it, it beat me again. I was already weakened from earlier. He threw me at the same place where my friends were.

He then encased us all inside a bubble of the emperor's pressure.

"Ugh, I guess they don't make warriors how they used to anymore. It was fun fighting you, but it's time to call it."

Sela tried rushing forward again, the wind in the barrier cut into his face making it look as his skin got peeled.

"Your face!" the emperor laughed, "Oh, sorry, I forgot to warn you. I wouldn't try passing through the field I placed you on. You'd be torn to shreds, but I guess you already know that. Nothing can penetrate that field. Speaking of penetration…"

The emperor walked towards Shamain. She tried fighting back with her pets, but he beat each down with ease her down to the ground. Shamain's dragon flew in on her defense. The dragon bit the emperor on the shoulder, but the emperor's might was too much. He landed a flurry of hits on the creature, breaking all of its mystic bones. The pain was felt in Shamain's core. The emperor had turned into a demon. He knocked Shamain down, and he got on top of her. The more Shamain resisted, the harder the emperor hit her. The emperor looked at me.

"Ah yes, I can see the pain in your eyes. Does it hurt brother, to see your sweet love getting violated? Ah, she is so soft. What would you say that this is what I do to her every night, and she loves it. Aw, come on, relax. Just look at it from the bright side, there is nothing you can do, so enjoy the show because this is bound to last!"

My hands were trembling. My eyesight was getting clouded in rage.

I slashed at the barrier, only to have it drain the sword's energy. The shine on the sword got dim.

"This field is draining our energy, fast. The more the struggle, the quicker the spell works" Umaso said.

"There has to be some way to break this seal. I can't just sit here and watch."

I slashed at the barrier. I was feeling light headed. Shamain's screams were breaking me down.

"I can't just give up here. I can't let this world be ruled by this sadistic asshole. I can't let Shamain be treated like this any longer!"

"Then fight" Sela said between heavy breaths "Right until the very end, ride this bitch until you or the enemy falls."

I felt Sela's energy flowing through me. Gaya and Umaso's light was shining on me now.

'Take my power as well' I heard Shamain whisper through her telecom

"Go" Gaya said. There was a sad smile on her face.

'I will pass onto you the last ounces of power that I have left. Your friends can see the true potential in you. You are the Hero of the Sword."

"Thank you"

I gripped onto the sword again. The renewed surge of energy I felt was as if the heavens had opened up to me. The sword grew massive, and it shone brighter than ever. The angels on the sword had come to life.

I charged ahead while clamoring a war cry. I stormed through the barrier; I felt the wall peeling off my skin and clothing. I gripped on the sword with everything I had left. All my feelings were concentrated at the tip of my sword; focused on changing everything for a brighter future.

The emperor noticed my attack. He let out another blast of pressure, but it was cut short thanks to Shamain's dragon which bit the emperor on his shoulder. I cut through the blast, and I plunged the sword into his mouth. He was prostrated there, unable to move.

"Shamain, get away from here. I don't know what will happen after the Demon King artifact is destroyed" I said. Her face was covered in tears (now I am free from you). "Sorry it took me so long"

That was my one moment of pure bravery.

She got up and hugged me and kissed me on the cheek before she went to aid my friends' escape leave the room. I didn't complain, but her touch, even her kiss, was painful;my skin had been shaven off. The emperor was in his knees. He tried fighting back with more energy blasts, but I didn't budge.

"Hey, Sela you punkass, get moving yes?!" I yelled at him from a distance.

"Do you always have to be naked?" Gaya shouted at me

"Babe, there's just no better way to feel the world right?" I replied

"Can you hold the emperor for fifteen minutes until we get out?" Umaso asked

"What?!"

"Just kidding, just give us thirty seconds"

"Yes sir captain commander!"

My friends exited.

'This is the task that was given since before I was born. I must do this alone. I will trade places with you. In return, please take good care of her.'

I stared at the fallen emperor's eyes while he was in a pathetic position, helpless. I stared at him for what it seemed an eternity. I felt my skin burn in my own determination. Then, I drove the sword straight from his mouth to his torso. I felt the jewel crack and then shatter.

'... You damn artifact, in fairy tales you are known as the Heaven's Stone. You trade one life for one wish. Now, grant me mine... Sorry Malak, I could never go back to you...'

Chapter 22 -- *Another World*

I my mind I knew I was certainly dead. No way that I could be alive after seeing that bright white light. It all made sense really, being at the epicenter of all ethereal energy and have that shit blow up meant complete disintegration. I would have died with my friends in battle. Somehow I cheated death once again.

I have no recollection on how I got here. My mind had gone completely blank; it was as though I seized to exist for a long time. Well, for as long time can be for someone who doesn't exist can remember. And then, I suddenly gained conscience of being alive, as if I had arrived back to the land of the living. For the longest moment I remember I could not see anything, move or feel. Everything was black, but somehow I knew I existed.

One day I opened my eyes. It was like I was born again. Almost literally actually: I could not talk; my sight was not good; I didn't have motor control, so I needed assistance just getting fed; I could not get up or walk; and I had a tube up my ass that would collect all my excrements -- most of the time I wasn't even aware I was shitting myself, zero vowel control. The nurses would always smile at me, and some would laugh rather suspiciously. I would later on find out they were calling me 'shit stained dick boy' and things like that. I was upset at the fact that I would never get the pretty nurses to give me baths touching me with their soft hands; in retrospective though, I am glad.

When I arrived in this world I could not speak. I didn't know the language. Slowly I learned through kindergarten books how to talk, read, and write. But the strange part was that I had lost the ability to speak my own native tongue. It took me a while before I could remember what my friends' names were --or at least how they sounded like.

So it took me a while to figure out where I was and to be able to speak to my own family. Apparently I had a mother and a sister -- considerably younger than I. When I first saw them they were full of tears of joy, and my mom would yell at me, but I didn't know what she was saying. Well, that hasn't changed since -- the yelling part and the lack of sense.

Apparently I had been in a comma for a long time. It had been some freak accident four years prior while I was riding my skateboard. I thought it was some epic trick I was trying to pull off, but when I read the report I found out that I was trying to pull an Ollie over a curb at a high speed. Not only did I miss, but the skateboard was vertical when I landed, so the board was rammed into my perineum. The theory is that I lost sense of vision of a small fraction of time, on which I managed to fall over a flight of stairs. I managed to soften the fall with my head as it seems. Also, I fell onto a bedding of glass at the end; I got multiple injuries from that. The report said that I was alone at the time. I am now twenty seven years old.

I didn't have a friend with me at the time of my accident, and I have had no friends come visiting me during my recovery. If I had any, I couldn't blame them if they didn't know I was alive. I was considered dead for quite a while, and people move on. The massive head trauma had altered something in my brain to the point that --according to the doctors-- it was as though my brain got formatted, making my brain the same as a newborn child's. So in short, chances for me to ever wake up were close to none. The only reason why I was kept alive is because my mom had never given up on me. She had spent a fortune keeping me alive.

Though I have no friends anymore, I am fine with this new start in life. And the reason why I am fine with it is because I had been building up a friendship with a girl that comes to visit the hospital often as a volunteer. Her name is Haba. She is gorgeous that girl. She has the softest hands I had ever felt. And her presence and smile make me giggle like a little kid. Granted, she talks to me because it is part of her

141

duties, so I should be careful before jumping in and let my impulses develop feelings that could end up getting me in a situation I wouldn't want to live again. But I don't know. I know we have developed some kind of meaningful presence since she spends more time with me than others, and she comes by every now and then outside her normal hours. None of that means she likes me in a boyfriend/girlfriend type of way, but as I keep hearing from my physical trainer 'no guts, no glory, and no apple pie'.

As I was relearning how to speak; one of the first things that I asked people was where Atlas tower was. At first, I figure that I should still be in the Empire's capital even though there was no sign of the tower. But people had no idea what I was saying. Nurses were starting to add 'crazy' or 'demented' as an extra adjective to my many nicknames. The doctor told me that all those memories were a fabrication of my mind while I was in a comma. He then added that since there are certain things science has yet to figure out about how exactly the brain works -- especially when it comes to conscience and memories -- that this Atlas world, with seemingly real people, could be a distortion of my brain.

I won't lie, I believed him for a good moment. And it saddened me to think everything that had happened was nothing but a figment of my own delusional comatose imagination. When I brought up parts about the lifestyle in Atlas, and the doctor would always have an answer to anything I said. He said those friends I knew were alterations of people I knew before I fell down the stairs. The whole BES concept was probably caused because of all the glass that I got jammed inside me. Everything else was explained with the simple answer that I had spent many hours watching anime movies and playing video games. And the biggest 'coincidence' of all was that in both of these worlds, my name is Jack.

When I did my research, there was no mentioning of the Empire's existence. I found countless of other empires that existed before this time, but nothing about the world that I lived in. The only thing that resembled my time was the story of the Tower of Babel. But other than the tower, there was no other concise linking to this story. Maybe it's the legend of Atlantis? But these stories are about thousands of years in the past. And the way I saw this world, civilization seemed to have moved hundreds of years in the past. Almost everything about this new world was primitive in comparison. These things, cellular phones, people are hooked to these things with dear life. I wonder how they'd be if they had a *telecom trinket.* The trinkets of my time could accomplish every task a personal computer could, and trinkets never had battery issues. At least these video games are quite entertaining. That's one thing we didn't have.

Regardless, all that mattered to me was that the world I was in, the life I had, was all gone. Hell, all the powers I once had were all gone too, and instead I spent a lot of painful hours learning how to walk again. And my friends, I was glad I was able to say good bye to them, but it didn't feel like it was enough. They could be in another planet, millions of light years away, but I knew I would never see them ever again.

At least I had my volunteering spiritual nurse who came to visit me every now and then like the angel she is. And one of my wishes finally came true. I have a family now. I have a mother who gave it all for me, and though most of the time she doesn't show it, but she loves me to no end. I have a sister, too. She does nothing but surround me with her love and admiration -- not sure if admiration is the right word, I haven't done anything but lie on a bed, but oh well, seems like it is impossible to understand women even if they are related to you by blood. My father is around as well, but my parents are divorced. Theirs marriage was rather unhappy, so it was for the best I guess. Haven't gotten to see my dad much, and the few times we met, we didn't really talk much, but I could see I had a part of his heart. Though I lost so much, I got such a loving family. I am happy. Did I mention that my favorite nurse is coming over soon?

... There are some nights when I stay awake thinking about this body I am in. I know it is not mine. Though the spirit that once owned this body was long gone, what if this other Jack wants to claim back is place?... But then I remember Sela, seeing him in Malak's camp, despite all his inner war, he fought hard and never looked back, and he smiled. I guess this is how it feels to fight new demons.

Before I met Haba, for a long time, I believed what the doctors said. Without being able to prove anything about the Empire, I really thought it was a product of being in a comma. But then one day I was being transferred to another room, I checked one of the drawers on the bedside table. In there I found my telecom trinket. Not sure how it got there. It didn't have much power left, and since I could not channel ethereal energy anymore, it would stop working soon -- not that it would be of any use in this world. The trinket showed I had a new message in. Strange enough, though I could not use my old language any longer, I understood what it was saying.

I can see Haba talking to one of the other nurses at a distance. She is thirty minutes early today. I leave the hospital in a week, hopefully then I will be able to ask her on a proper date. I see her looking over at me now. I can't believe I am having such a hard time tuning down my smile. Ah well, I guess I will close these chapters in my book now. It's time for me to start a new one.

Chapter 23 -- *a Telecom Message*

MESSAGE START

Dear Jackie,

This is Sonja. You did it! I don't know how, but you finished your mission. You know I don't normally say this, but thank you. I lost my LWS during the siege. Alon came to my rescue, but he got injured in the process. It wasn't too bad though, we were holding hands and then he told me he loved me. Yes, I know you want to hear all about it. The suit had been pushed to its limits, and it was about to explode. With demons at every angle, and no place to go, we knew that we were dead. But then, a bright flash of light came from the tower, flooding everything. Right at that moment without any delay, every demon turned to dust, and the Leatonian core seized to function.

From the reports that Gaya received, the light covered the entire world. And in all over the world, ethereal ores lost their glow. My weapons do not work any longer, but my telecom trinket still works though I can see it losing its life. The core of the tower is still emitting a light, but its source has been unresponsive to any stimuli. I don't know for how much longer the light will keep emitting; the tower itself is starting to break apart.

I do not know why I am writing you this, I guess it's because we all miss you. Umaso said that when he went back to the Imperial House, there was no sign of you; as if you had just vanished. The Mighty Hunter had been turned into a disfigured stone statue. A hunk of rusted metal was planted on the statue's mouth. That, and there was a naked man lying on the floor. He is very tall and handsome. I hear he is the Hero of the Sword. His name is Sui Renshi.

I feel like I need to tell you this. I know that you liked that girl Shamain, but she has been with Sui Renshi ever since he appeared. That guy is quite muscular, and he is incredibly handsome. Sorry. At least she looks happy. I would be.

Speaking of friends; I guess you want to know about Sela as well. He lost his demon scars, and those demons of his seem to have gone away. He looks quite handsome without his scars, but he is such a dick! How are you friends with this guy?

Umaso decided to keep the name you knew him by. Gaya and he send you their greetings. I think they would have liked you to be at their wedding. I think Umaso would have made you the best man. You were the one that got them back together after all. By the way, did you have a thing for Gaya? It just looked that way. Ugh, I wish you were here. I am so curious! Which reminds me; why in the hell did you shoot Gaya? Sometimes Jackie, I have no idea what goes in your head.

Well, if anyone misses you the most is Malak. She is very cute! Way to go there champ! And she is very nice, too. They decided to come back to help the people adapt to the new life without ethereal energy. Malak and I have become good friends; she is right next to me actually. She is asking me to tell you this:

'Jackie --my love-- how are you? I miss you so much. My/our daughter misses you too. I just want to say thanks for all the good times. Like the day you took care of me when I got sick with, you know. I just want to see you so much. I think of you all the time. Sometimes I wish that I would have had your child before you left. I wish I had a picture of us together, holding hands. Though I am mad that you didn't keep your promise, I understand. I will always love you no matter what. You love me too right? Wherever you are, I just hope that you find a good woman. But hopefully she is not pretty, so that you will always think of me. Baby, if you can, please come back to me.'

Sorry, she left. The poor girl loves you so much, and you just went and left; you're such a bastard.

Anyways, I still remember the day that we first met. I went to see Umaso, and you were standing next to him. You looked so cute the way you were so scrawny. And then you didn't say hello and you just came to hug me, and then out of nowhere you started humping me. Oh boy, I remember that day like yesterday. I think you got a boner no? I couldn't really tell since you probably have a small dick. I know you want me.

Well, we are all here now, moving on with our lives. For some reason different towns are starting to speak in different languages. Inside the city even, there are some that have started to pick on a new language. People are starting to spread out with those they can talk to. I won't lie to you. You left a mess behind. Thanks. Well, I guess it wouldn't be good old Jackie if he didn't leave his piss mark in this world right?

I guess I will stop now. I just hope that one day I will hear from you. I just refuse to believe that you are dead. You have so much more to do, like getting married and having kids. It would be very funny to see little Jackies running around while you start losing your...

MESSAGE END

Appendix

Appendix A -- an Explanation on Ethereal Magic

When the Mighty Hunter conquered the demon, people received the ability to use *magic [ethereal energy]*. This ability was granted to the people of the Hunter's tribe. But as the empire spread, a small number of people that were born from parents without magic abilities could be born with the gift. This strange event happened only from one in a thousand. So, only descendants from the original tribe, and those "lucky" few were able to use these powers. The only other rare cases of people that are able to use *magic* were those who had demon ancestors, like Sela.

A *magic* user couldn't use these powers with his life--force alone. The user had to be close to a *source*. The very first sources were the weapons that were blessed by the heavens in the slaying of the demon beast. These were very rare, and the few remaining were used by royalty.

The most common source used in the Empire was crystals that were manufactured in the Tower of Unity -- the center of *magic* powers. These crystals powered everything in the empire: they provided from the most basic needs such as lighting and hot water to being the power source for space stations. The generating capacity of the Tower was almost limitless.

But there was one more engineering problem with these crystals. The crystals were useless if they were too far outside of the Tower's range. For this problem, the tower grew as tall as it was to reach the ends of the world.

In order for space travel to be possible, the Empire developed portals that connected the Tower with each mother ship. These mother ships acted as the Tower would in outer space. This technology was relatively new, and it was starting to replace the use of crystals in other large applications.

Another source was gathered from demons. Their body parts possessed similar qualities as the crystals, but unlike these, demon parts did not need to be in contact with the Tower. The main disadvantage of demon parts is that they were not as efficient as the crystals. Demon parts were used mainly in manufacturing small arms and other personal military gear.

There were two types of personal weapons that could be made: melee, and projectile weapons. The melee weapon could range from anything from knuckles, to massive pole arms. It was the most basic tool for any magic user. Though it was possible to activate *magic* with a bare hand as long as a source was nearby; to fully make effective use of our abilities, we needed the aid of a close--range weapon.

The second type was the projectile weapons, more commonly known as hand cannons. These were basically as the name implies; a portable cannon. There was a magic embedded crystal shard embedded at the end of base of the barrel. The user would charge the crystal, and then shoot a large ball of energy. To increase damage, the user could also insert *enchanted* ammo into the barrel. Hand cannons were particularly difficult to use because it took a lot of energy to charge the crystal, but they were deadly efficient. These cannons were mainly made with a single barrel, but I had seen ones with as many as four barrels. The more barrels, the more difficult it was to use the weapon. Barrel length also affected the gun's power.

In short, when thinking of a *magic* user and the *source;* think of the user as a battery, and the *source* as a radio. The Tower would be the broadcasting station.

Gaya was quite the savage eater. By the time she was done, her side was messier than mine. And my side was quite messy, too.

"Hmm, it's delicious, I am so full now!" by now Gaya had eaten all the money that I had been saving for my trap. I wasn't sure how I was going to pay for this one; she had eaten more than her usual!

Watching her eat was quite the event. My hangover was killing me.

"What!" she yelled "You were staring at me weren't you. Gosh, I don't like it when you do that. You look like such a pervert! Jack, I think you like me."

My eyes opened wide when she said that, and my face was getting hot.

"No..." I had no idea what to say.

"You know, I think I am falling in love." She said it softly.

"Really, who is this person?"

"I am falling for you" She said it even softer.

Now, I was clearly red like a tomato, and my chest was pumping. But this was my moment; I couldn't get a better set up. I had to tell her about my feelings for her, now.

"I... I..." I started stuttering. The words were in my head, but I couldn't control my mouth.

"Just kidding!" she said. What a letdown.

"So, you couldn't see yourself with me?" I tried to say it casually while catching my voice back.

"Maybe..." her voice broke a little bit "But no way! I could never be with you like that."

"Ok, so what if I liked you?"

"No because we're friends. Friends don't do that." She was getting serious.

So much for my decision to tell her I liked her. I should just wait for another time.

"Gaya, I really like you" I said. "As in, I really do."

Stupid, I shouldn't have said anything, she pretty much told me 'no' just a moment ago.

"Jack, don't say things like that. We are only friends, ok? Just friends" Now she was pissed.

Things got uncomfortably quiet. I messed things up, so I tried to lighten the mood.

"How about in another life, what if I rose up in the [military] ranks and I made a lot of money?"

She smiled.

"Then I'll marry you for sure, and you can buy me lots of clothes and jewelry, and lots of food from different places in the world. You know, I really love..." she paused, and started to sniff the air "Did you just fart? Oh my... this is why you're single! You're so nasty!"

"It wasn't intentional..." My face got white.

She got ready to leave "Just for that you're paying -- Bye!"

At least I lightened the mood. But now I had to figure out how to pay the bill --which the waiter handed it to me while covering his nose with his hand.

That day I got lucky. I was way too late. So the disciplinary head cut the punishment short. I only got a couple of bumps in my head, so I could hide them with my hair. I wanted to be presentable for my lady. What did I like about her? I don't know. She was pretty, but more than that, she always seemed happy and full of life. She did things her own way, and that always intrigued me.

After I got my beating -- and my new class schedule -- I still had time to attend my first class of the day. I was hoping that Liora wasn't in that class. I wasn't ready to see her yet.

My first class was with Mr. Ham. He was a man of legend, a hero of our empire. It is said that he and his squadron had once stopped a large underground terrorist group and their plot to take over the world. Hey, I said the land was in peace, but seldom there were rebels. Back then I never understood what their purpose was.

Mr. Ham was also famous for his skills in both melee and ranged weapons, and he was also known for his ability in combat tactics. He was the super soldier we all hoped to become. On top of that, he was also one of the most sought out bachelors in the community. He was loved by the students, especially the girls. Sometimes I could hear them talking about him, and how they wondered how come he never married. Maybe he hadn't found the right woman? My best guess was that he had commitment issues. I just envied the bastard.

"Yes, this is the right class" Mr. Ham said as soon as I stuck my head out in the classroom's door.

After I got spotted, I made my way to my seat hoping to not cause too much of a disturbance. It was a small classroom; it probably couldn't seat more than twenty five students. The place was filled with so many familiar places. Luckily,

Liora wasn't one of them. As I looked through the desks, I noticed that my dearest friends had actually saved me a seat. Strange, they couldn't bother waking me up, but they did save me a seat.

Sela had the audacity to ask me, as if he didn't know "Where were you all morning?"

"Sleeping" I said "Where else do you think I have been?! I can't believe you just left me."

"Well, we did try waking you up, you weren't. I even kicked you. You probably have a weld from it." said Alon, who was seating behind me.

It was a believable argument, I do sleep like a rock, and I couldn't sleep the night before. Later on I checked my hip, and he was right; I had large a weld with the shape of Alon's foot.

Alon and Sela were my two closest friends. Unlike me, they were strong. I had pretty much grown up with them since very young, especially Alon. When we grew up that he always had my back countless of times. That punkass, there were a couple of times when kicked my ass, too. I remember that he was always the clever kid. You could never turn your back from him because if you weren't paying attention he could have sold your soul to you and you wouldn't notice. Not many people could beat him on a verbal fight.

Other than that, Alon would get your respect right from the start. You could see a certain strength coming from Alon, and if you didn't know him, he could strike you as a very intimidating man. He had a very short temperament to boot. If you ever saw Alon getting red, you had better back up. Not even Sela -- who was the stronger of the two -- liked to mess with Alon in his *red hot rage* mode. I was the one who gave him that nickname. He kicked my ass for it --he disliked being told that he had anger issues -- and then he kicked my ass once again after the name stuck.

153

Sela was the more impressive of the two. The first thing you'd notice was this third arm on his right side -- his birth mark. He was born half human, half demon -- a half--breed. He sure had a tough childhood. He got picked on by kids and adults alike for being born "inferior." He got in countless of fights because of it. But there was nothing inferior about Sela; he was very strong. He had never lost a fight, and I had yet to see him use his full strength. That third arm of his was no decoration; he could use it very well.

He barely ever used his demon abilities for fighting purposes. But one of the things he could do was to make as many arms come out of his body, and he could make more arms come out from the arms without much effort --so he had quite the reach. It was the power that he inherited from his own bloodline. But he preferred to use his power for other purposes. He liked to grab girls with his arms. Yes, Sela was quite charming with women. More than his strength I admired his ease with girls the most. To this day it's still a mystery to me how he could get the attention of so many girls. I tell you this though: from my years of observation I noticed that women are unexplainably attracted to men who've slept around a lot, while men don't care.

The bell rang not long after I sat down. I then realized that maybe I could have saved myself from a beating if I had come to school after lunch; which is when we were allowed to leave the academy.

"And tomorrow we will be analyzing field tactics, so don't forget to bring your plans for case 587. Remember, these are graded."

"Are you kidding me? We have cases already?" I couldn't believe it.

"Yes young man, make sure you get your notes from one of your friends." Apparently the Mr. Ham overheard me. He also had very keen ears.

I wouldn't have been bombed so much about the homework, but when it came to field cases, we had to think about everything: location of the nearest safe point, possible dangers of the land, weather, etc. It always took me all night to figure them out.

"Well, let's get out of here" said Sela, "you'll catch up later, but first we got some more important news to keep up with."

"Have you heard of the new girl from the West Islands?" said Alon.

 I had no idea who that new girl was.

"Anyways, her name is Shamain, she's pretty good looking; you might like her."

I wasn't very interested in some new girl, and my faced showed my lack of interest. My friends knew why.

"So, I bet you're waiting to see Miss Tits, huh?" Sela was right on target, and yes her boobs were phenomenal. "When are you going to ask that girl out? It is the last year you know."

"I know, and can you please stop calling her that?" I replied quickly and unwelcoming of the comment "I am just waiting for the right moment this time. Just wait and see, I'll ask her."

They didn't believe though; I wouldn't have either.

"You know Jack; there is never 'the' right time for these kinds of things." Sela went on "You just have to man up, start talking to her, and then you ask her out. It's that simple"

He was right, but he wasn't the type of guy who would freeze in front of a girl.

Alon started to laugh at my torment "Hey Sela, do you remember the annual party three years ago"

"Oh yeah, it was hilarious, I remember Jack's face when Liora kissed him."

"It was just on the cheek, too. If I had been in your situation, I would have started making out with her right away."

"How did that night go again? Right, we were going to the party…"

I remember how they just loved to bring that old topic back again every time they could. It never got old for them. But I rather tell you in my own words what had happened.

Four years prior, we were going to the school's annual party. It was the first party that I was able to go to. I didn't know what to expect from it. I was just hoping it would be a fun time. We were all walking in groups towards the party. In my group there was Sela -- who was busy flirting in the back of the group -- Alon was to my right, and Liora was on my left, with her friends. I didn't have any interest in Liora at the time -- I didn't even know who she was until then since I had just gotten into the academy. So, while Liora was talking, she made a joke that I didn't find funny. I can't remember what she said, but I started to laugh loudly as if I cared about her conversation. Instead of finding me offensive, for some reason Liora found that funny.

She looked at me and then she said "How cute, I could marry you right now." and then she then kissed me on the cheek, twice.

All I can remember is that I was speechless, rather petrified. I remember reacting very strange that night. I never said anything back to her that night, or any other time since then. I was charmed from a kiss --in the cheek. I was young; I had never been interested in a particular girl before then. I was interested in the female anatomy yes, but not someone specific. I had never had someone liking me, or saying that she liked me. I didn't know what to do. I felt so naked that night. It was quite sad.

My friends were laughing their lungs off.

"And everyone saw you." Alon kept reminding me about that night for about an eternity.

For some strange reason I turned to him, and punched him as hard as I could in the front of his shoulder -- right at the gleno--humeral joint. It is the area between the deltoid and the pectoral muscles. You should try it on your friends. But expect them to react violently. --

Alon did get pissed. The second I hit him he got red.

"You're dead" he said, but I already knew that.

I started to run as fast as I could, but I knew that Alon would eventually catch me, so I tried to run towards a populated area in hopes of saving myself. I headed to the student patio.

Through the crowd I noticed that Liora was there. I couldn't believe my eyes, she looked so beautiful. It was as though she kept getting prettier every year. No, she kept getting better every minute, every second. My heart was pounding uncontrollably. It felt as though I was losing control of my vowels. This is why I couldn't talk to her all these years. I used to get so nervous in her presence.

But I should not have forgotten about my surroundings. Big mistake, Alon was still after me, and his famous *butt tackle* brought me back to reality.

The *butt tackle* is not a move you should be trying on your friends unless you don't mind risking injuring them. Basically the person using this tackle runs towards the target and then jumps with a one eighty degree turn. The point of contact on the target is your rear end. For maximum effectiveness, the impact hits on the target's upper shoulder or neck. To increase damage, the target's back should be facing you so that it works like a sneak attack. Alon could use this move to perfection.

All I could remember after I focused my eyes on Liora is that a second later I was flying through the area lifting up debris while rolling on the floor.

"Oh yeah, now get ready for the pain!" Alon's bully instinct was kicking in, but then he noticed I was immobile "Jack?"

"I think you over did it" said Sela, as he helped me get back up. "Hold on, there is someone I have to see. I'll be right back." His playboy nature had kicked in, so he did what he had to do.

"Sorry Jack" said Alon, "but why did you stop running?" He looked to the side and noticed Liora, so he found out by himself before I said anything. "I see, well you should at least talk to her; it's the last year you know?" He looked to his side "There's Gaya. I'm going to catch up with her, so I'll see you later"

"Gaya? Who's that?" I asked

Alon looked at me surprised "What? You know who she is! She's right there!"

For some reason I couldn't remember who Gaya was.

I noticed a girl, a little shorter than me, walking towards us. She then greeted me.

"Hey Jack! How you've been?"

As soon as I heard that uncomfortable sound resonating in my eardrums I finally remembered who the owner of that boyish voice was. It was Gaya. She was nice enough to try talking to me a number of times before, but I was inexplicably rude to her. I didn't hate or even dislike her, but it was as though every part of her invited me to be a total ass towards her. So I replied nonchalantly.

"Oh, good, great, goodbye" I dismissed her.

Obviously that upset her "What the hell is wrong with you?! Why... Whatever." Then she left with Alon who didn't know what to think of my reaction.

Gaya was nothing more than a punching bag for me back then, but eventually I got to know her. It took me a while to notice how beautiful she was. Where could I start to describe her? I could say that anyone who met her would agree in one thing; she was quite the memorable character. She was the type of person whose charisma attracted those around her. She was really outgoing and wild, spontaneous, and at times she was loud, very loud. At first I found it annoying, but then I found that quite charming about her. Also, she could eat like a beast.

I had to do something about Liora. The pressure was building. I thought, if only I could build the confidence to talk to her. I had no idea what I would say to her. I had come up with countless of things I could say over the years, but none of them were good. It was my personal oath to do whatever it took to go out with her, but I was already three years behind. Sela was right, it was now or never

Liora was now sitting alone. It was the perfect moment. Her two bodyguards were nearby as usual, but they weren't going to do anything if I approached her. I knew that Liora was one of a descendant from the original tribe, but aside from that I didn't know much else. I tried getting closer to her, but what would I say? Soon enough my nerves got the best of me, and I just couldn't do it. Next time I was going to do it, yes next time.

As I turned around in defeat, I noticed an unfamiliar face standing in front of me, dressed a bit differently from what I was used to. She was extremely beautiful. I knew from her looks she was not from around here. She was thin and tall, gracious in her movement. You could see a certain strength hidden beneath her delicate frame. Her pale grey eyes were deep. It was as though she could see inside me. Instead of feeling threatened, I welcomed it. She was gorgeous.

159

"Hello" she said "my name is Shamain."

I was charmed from the beginning "Hi, I'm Hadassah. But since I can tell we are going to be friends, just call me Jack, like my friends do." Strange, I had no problems talking to her.

"Jack" she said my name with her sweet voice "cute."

"I heard about you, you're the new girl from the West Islands right? What brings you to the central city?"

"I always wanted to see the city, so I decided to transfer here."

"Wow that must have been a long journey. I bet you miss your boyfriend."

"What boyfriend?" she said it in a serious tone.

"Oh, I thought you have one since, well, since you are so…" I paused "charming"

She was just looking at me, so I quickly tried to change the subject "But don't worry, I will keep you company while you are here."

"Sure" she smiled at me, and what a smile. "You must be quite a charming guy with girls."

"No, not at all really, there is something about you…"

I couldn't believe I was having such ease talking with this beautiful girl. But like with anything great the conversation came to an abrupt end. Sela showed up behind me.

"Hey Jack, aren't you going to present me to your girlfriend?" *damn you* "hello, my name is Sela, nice to meet you"

"I'm Shamain, nice meeting you, too"

Sela went in for a hug. A traditional move he used a lot.

"Where did Alon go?"

"He left to meet with…" I couldn't remember her name again

"Gaya" at least Sela knew her name "Figures. Well, let's go eat"

"Sure, *(party pooper)*" I didn't want our meeting to end, so I turned to Shamain "would you like to join us?"

"No, it's ok. I have to go meet with a teacher. Maybe next time, ok? It was nice meeting you though."

As soon as she left, I knew what was coming.

"Dude, that girl is hot. If you don't ask her out, I will." I knew he would, too.

"Come on man, it's not like that. And can you just let her be?"

"Oh! I knew it, your digging that girl, huh? Telling you dude; just ask her out, I bet she'll say yes."

"Ok, let's say I ask her out, where would I ask her out to?"

"Do I have to think about that, too?" he was getting into it "What about you ask her to join us next time we go hunting? Listen; let me give you a tip. If you can grab the girl's leg, there shouldn't be a problem for you to get her in bed. Once you can grab the girl's leg; that means she is comfortable with you, so you're in good shape. Am telling you; just let her do the talking. Women love talking. There is no day that a woman is in no mood for some yabbing…" and on and on.

What a day.

Appendix D -- *Demon Hunting*

We didn't have many free days during school times. But
when we did, one of my favorite activities to do with my
friends was *demon hunting*. We would go out of the limits
of the city to remote lands where giant beasts wandered the
land. It was part of our training and our duty to the empire.
These beasts were spawns of demons that raped the fauna.
These beasts destroyed everything on their path, and they
had no place in this earth.

Demon hunting was also a spectacle event for the masses. It
was such a popular activity that there was a professional
league of hunters. Being a hunter was also an alternate
lifestyle that you could choose, but you had to be good at it.
Sela was already good enough to join the pro ranks.

These beasts varied in appearance, but they were all
gigantic. You could see the muscles popping out of their
skin. Some of them had horns the size of my body, and
some had fangs that were full of poison. Though they
weren't very smart; they were not creatures to take lightly.
We didn't just hunt these beasts for training and keeping the
balance in the wild environments, but these beasts also
possessed the materials that were fundamental in the making
of *enchanted* weapons.

Our gear was limited to our personal weapons, magic bombs
and traps, whatever we could carry without our *magic bags*.
We also wore rudimentary armor that was made from
various parts of these demons; nothing else worked as well
when facing them.

It was always an adventure when going in these hunts. It
always brought me peace. I almost never went hunting
without Sela though. One day I had gone with only Alon.
We couldn't work well as a team, and we almost died.

That day it was me, Alon and Sela out in the fields. Sela brought a girl with him to join us. The more the merrier. I didn't bring any extra companions with me. I hadn't asked Liora out yet, and I hadn't seen much of Shamain since.

Alon came by himself as well. I hadn't seen much of Alon him during the past weeks since he was busy with Gaya. He was very upset that day. We were still at the safety post, a place where groups gathered before the hunt.

"What is wrong?" I asked Alon "I thought you were bringing that girl along."

Alon didn't seem to want to tell me at first, but then he spoke. "We got into a fight"

"You two seemed fine to me. Well, except for the public fights"

"I know; we've had our arguments. But this just isn't right" Alon was getting annoyed by the thought "I think she is going to break it between us. I don't know I just have a bad feeling"

"I don't know what to tell you. Sorry."

"It's ok; I don't want to talk about it. Let me get ready for the hunt." Alon got up and he was focused on prepping his gear.

I never understood very well how people tend to change their hearts. It was somewhat a mystery to me. I wondered if I ever got with Liora, if she would change her heart as well. I certainly hoped she wouldn't.

"Are you ready Sela?" I asked.

"Yes, just give me a minute. Are you ready babe?" he asked his girl

"No, it's ok. I'll just wait for you here. I have some to get ready for an exam next week." She replied in a girly voice.

You could just tell Sela was starting to get upset. I would have, too. How could you come to hunting grounds and not hunt? Sela tried to convince her to join, but to no avail. So he dismissed her.

"Alright guys, ready."

"Oh yes, definitely" I said in excitement. The thrill of the hunt was too much to bear, but all my emotions would come to a halt very soon.

On the distance, at the other side of the post I noticed Liora. But she was not alone. She was with some other guy. They were holding hands with their fingers intertwined the other. She then leaned over to his side, and then they kissed.

The three of us were all ready to head into the fields. The mission was to hunt this demon beast that had been tormenting a nearby population. From what we could gather from the people that had seen the beast was that it looked a lot like a giant cock rooster, and it liked to hide in the woods nearby.

We weren't the only ones on this mission. There were other groups assigned to the task, including Liora's. The first group to catch the demon was the one getting the reward.

The demon we had to hunt for the day was a low--profile monster, so it didn't attract much attention. It didn't matter for Alon though. His eyes were set in destroying something. To aid him on this task, he was carrying his specialty weapon. It was a hybrid stave. It was a massive stave that was too heavy for me to handle, but this weapon was swift in Alon's hands. The pole was actually a barrel, and it could fire a massive projectile. Alon carried one handed axes as his secondary.

I was carrying my trusted short sword -- it was general issue. I had it since I was young, and for some reason no other weapon reacted better to my stimuli. I was also carrying my regular duty single barreled hand cannon. I was also carrying some ammo, bombs, and all the traps we would need. I was the one in charge of that.

Sela on the other hand was only carrying hand cannons, four of them in total: one large single handed cannon; two double barreled cannons; and a massive three barreled cannon --his favorite.

It took us a couple of hours to get to the target area. We set up camp, and while we were waiting we were going through our plans, but you could tell that the team synergy was off. Alon was quiet, but inside him there was rage building up. And I just couldn't concentrate. How could I? The girl of my dreams was with someone else, and to make things worse, she was nearby with that guy.

"Is everything ok?" Sela asked us both

"Yeah, I am ready" Alon replied on a serious tone. "Let's start. I'll go scout the area."

Sela turned to me "What is it Jack? You both seem off. Talk to me, did you two get in a fight?"

"No, he is upset about something with him and Gaya. I'm sure they'll be ok." I didn't think those two would really break up.

"Well, figures. What happened to you? You were ok a while ago. Is Liora isn't it? Well, right now isn't the time to let something like that to get you down"

"You're right. It's my fault I let that happen. I guess it was a matter of time." I paused for a second "I mean, who lets four years pass by like that?!" I was feeling very down.

"No, never heard of anyone doing that, but you." This was Sela trying to console me. "It is better if you forget about her. There are better girls out there. If you want I know of a place where we can go and meet some girls. And don't worry, I'll pay."

"Thanks, but it's ok; I just wanted to get to know her a bit better."

"Well, maybe you want to reconsider my offer [on meeting the girls]" Sela paused for a second "Did Alon take traps with him?"

"No, I have them with me." I stopped. I realized that Alon didn't go scouting. We didn't say a word. We hurried off to find Alon. Though Alon was strong, no demon beast was to be taken lightly.

It didn't take us long to track down Alon. You could hear the shrieking from the beast a mile away.

"You know the drill, get close and set the traps. Call Alon when you're ready. I'll go support." Sela yelled as we were running.

Soon after that Sela disappeared on my right through the bushes. I felt a bit disoriented because I visibility was really poor. The vegetation was getting extremely dense, but I could still hear the screeching of the demon getting louder. I knew I was getting closer because the booming screeches were getting loud to the point of it getting painful.

It was getting really hot running wearing my armor. The humidity was getting to me. I started to feel my body drenched in sweat. I was starting to get scared. If only the sound of the demon was this terrifying, then I could only imagine the power of it. I wanted to stop to take a breath, but I was starting to get worried about Alon.

I don't know how long I was had been running through the tall vegetation, but luckily I was able to grab sight of the demon. I was relieved to see Alon still fighting, but he did not seem to be in good shape; half of his armor was already torn. The descriptions of the demon were actually accurate though. It looked a lot like a chicken -- more like a battle cock to be exact.

What appeared to be a clearing was actually the landscape that had gotten destroyed in the hunt. As soon as I got inside the perimeter I installed my trap. Traps were devices designed for hunting. When triggered, they released an energy charge onto the target, and then it tangled it with a net -- quite handy, durable and reusable.

I shot at the demon chicken with my cannon to get its attention. As I did that I called out to Alon to lure the demon towards my side.

The bird followed, and fell for the trap. Its screeching was piercing my drums, and the trap didn't seem to be able to hold much longer.

"Move aside team! Let's do this!" Sela yelled out while aiming his four cannons at the chicken. He took a while because he had to charge his cannons to the max -- and he felt like climbing to the top of the highest tree; that show--off.

"SOORIA" he yelled out while he blasted the cannons at the demon.

And as usual, he overdid it. He caused a huge cloud of dirt to rise from the blast. And by the time the dirt settled, there was barely anything left from the chicken. He even destroyed my trap, so there went half of my month's allowance. Not like it mattered since I didn't have any dates.

Later on Alon admitted that Gaya had dumped him.

Appendix E -- *Shamain's Sadness*

I saw Shamain sitting at the courtyard. I hadn't seen much of her either. She looked sad.

I went to say hello, and then I asked why she looked so sad. She told me that she was missing her life back in the West Islands. I told her that she could count on me if she wanted to hang out. She smiled at me, but she didn't seem too happy with the idea.

"Can I get a hug" she requested all of a sudden.

"Of course" I didn't refuse. I remember when we hugged that I was blushing. No one had ever asked me for a hug before, at least not the way she did. Her tone was so sweet, and her scent was hypnotizing. I was mesmerized once again. But I could notice a deep sadness in her that I couldn't help take away.

Everyone knew what had happened the night before. We couldn't hide it; Gaya and I were covered in bruises. The right side of my face was swollen from the bitch--slap I got from the wraith. I never heard the end of it.

I was still confused about Shamain. I wanted to ask her what had happened in the barren lands, but I couldn't find her anywhere. It had been a week since the incident with the wraith, and she hadn't come to school ever since. I wondered if she had left school. Strangely, I had not told anyone about her little intervention.

There were more pressing matters going on at the moment though. Ever since the incident, Gaya and I were getting along better. Alon didn't seem too happy about that, and the fact that Sela kept bringing the idea of me liking her didn't help my cause either. And it's not like I felt that way about her either.

Ok, who am I kidding? I was starting to enjoy Gaya's company a bit too much. But I couldn't get myself to like her. I couldn't do this to Alon. Though Gaya and Alon had fallen off, I knew that Alon still liked her. Besides, their situation was still very tense. Gaya and I were just friends, and we could stay that way fine, right?

It was after school time once again.

"So I get what happened over at the barrens and the whole wraith thing and all. But come on tell me the truth, why was she there?" Sela said it with a little smirk "I'm just asking because you two seem to be getting along"

"Sela... for the fiftieth time; she just popped out of nowhere. She asked me why I kept blowing her off, and after that we were just chatting." It was quite uncomfortable to explain myself with Alon around. Something that Sela seemed to be enjoying quite a lot.

"Ah, so I get it. You were always brushing her off because you secretly liked her. That's ok, you didn't know either. A lot of relationships start that way." Sela was definitely enjoying this terrible moment.

I was clearly nervous now "Alon, seriously, nothing's going on between me and her."

"Oh, don't worry about it. I honestly don't care about what you two do." He was clearly lying. I knew him very well. Deep inside he was boiling in anger, and he was trying hard not to show it.

"Anyways" Alon continued "I have to get ready for exams, so I'll talk to you later." He lied again. Truth was that Gaya was coming over, so he decided to leave.

"So, it's none other than my friend's life saver" Sela said, in his usual smooth tone while he hugged Gaya. What a smooth bastard.

"Oh, no, Jack did his part, too. But not much just loaded with homework" she then turned to me "Hey Jack! What are you doing later? I am hungry. Have you eaten yet?" She ate quite a lot.

"Well, we can go eat in a bit if you want. I'll go with you" I said as plainly as possible.

"Great! Let me go drop my books off. I'll be back."

As soon as Gaya left, Sela was giving me that look. His suspicions were obvious.

"No, seriously, we're just friends!"

"You don't have to tell me anything" Right, his mind was already made up. "Well, go and have fun with her, I have to go take care of some other business." By that he meant he had to go and see his chick.

Sela left. So I was just watching Gaya going to drop off her stuff. Not sure when it started, but I couldn't get my eyes off her anymore. I was just watching her talking to the Big Cheese. He grabbed her arm.

"Hey! Let go of me!" Gaya yelled, clearly unhappy.

The Big Cheese, as his name says, was a huge kid even bigger than Sela. He hailed from the northern areas of the empire. He was younger than me, but he already looked like an adult. His hair was red, and he had massive patches of hair all over his body. Just like the people from where he comes from, he was strong. Cheese liked to use his massive strength to bully others. He never really bothered me though since I hung around Alon and Sela. The latter was the one who gave him the name of Big Cheese, he didn't seem to mind. I didn't even know his real name.

"Hey honey, easy, why don't you and I go and hang out instead, and leave this loser behind."

"No thanks" Gaya said while trying to get her arm loose.

"Come on, I'm pretty sure we're going to have a lot of fun."

"Sorry, but I am rather busy. Maybe some other time ok?"

"Busy with that loser you mean!" He was starting to get angry and jealous "So what, are you two hitting the sack already?"

I was feeling a bit brave from my confrontation with an actual wraith, so I decided to get in the mix.

"Hey! Leave her alone you fat ass." I interfered as if I was some hero.

"Why, are you going to stop me? Interesting, how do you plan to do that?"

"Damn right, so let go of her before I kick your ass!"

He pushed Gaya away and then he got up. I had forgotten how big he was, but I was confident I could take him on. My experience in the barrens was sure to pay off.

Cheese laughed at me. "I'll destroy your puny self and then rape you!"

He rushed towards me. I readied my fist. As soon as he was in my range I unleashed a massive uppercut charged with energy towards his jaw. I connected so well my knuckles were burning. I made sparks fly out of his chin.

It turns out all I did was scrape his skin. He then grabbed me by the arm, lifted me in the air and tossed me like a ragdoll. Damn it, I guess I was far from being strong.

I was screwed, so I rolled myself into a ball to receive the beating that was about to come. I didn't mind though, at least I stood up for Gaya, my friend, I sure she would appreciate that.

"I'm going to make you my girl now!" Cheese said, but then his tone changed "Oh no, wait!"

All I heard was the sound of a plethora of hits. When I looked over, Cheese just fell on the floor all bruised and battered. Sela had come back to land a beating on the Cheese.

"Now, what did I tell you about messing with my friends?" I have to give it to Sela; he had always had my back.

"Jackie, are you ok?" Sela said while he helped me up.

"What in the world made you think you could have faced that guy?" Gaya came over "I had it all taken care of"

Now I looked more like a fool than anything.

"Well, I thought I could take him on since I've improved since the barrens."

"It didn't look like that from what I saw." Sela said, laughing "Next time, you should just let the girl take care of you"

"Yeah" she agreed.

"Anyways, I will leave you two lovebirds go on and do your thing."

Gaya and I were blushing. Sela was really the blunt type of guy, and he enjoyed the awkward moments.

"Are you ok Jack?" Gaya asked in a concerned tone, but she soon changed it "Next time, don't try acting so macho. It really doesn't suit you. What were you thinking really?"

Oh wow "I mean, he was disrespecting you, and what else do you think I would have done?" I was getting frustrated.

"Well, you could have told him he was being immature" she actually said that "Well, you're paying for lunch now, thanks!"

Women

It was way past lunch time. That fat ass, all she liked to do was eat.

I wondered where Shamain had banished to. I looked for her, and I couldn't find her. It seemed so strange to me that neither Alon nor Sela had brought her up since the first day of classes. More so, during all this time Sela had never hit on Shamain, not even when I was spending all this time with Gaya. I wondered if she left, why she never said goodbye -- though it's not like we knew each other that well.

Time had passed, and it was now the last day of classes, most of the students would be gone after this, including my friends. I would stay a couple more weeks, waiting to be deployed into outer orbit.

I met Gaya at the student patio inside the school.

"Where were you?" Gaya said "I've been looking for you everywhere."

"Hey, I went to say my greetings to Mr. Ham. I am glad I found you though." I said.

"So, you're graduating…" she paused. "Well, congratulations!"

"Thank you." I didn't know what to say. I had so many things I wanted to tell her, but nothing was coming out.

"I guess I won't be seeing you after this, huh?" Her face saddened.

"I know, but maybe someday we will meet again." I couldn't smile either.

We were quiet for a while. I never wanted it to end. I was trying to think of something, to talk about something else so that our last moment together wouldn't be so shitty. Then I got a brilliant idea.

"Hey Gaya, listen. Maybe when you graduate we can keep in touch once you get your *telecom trinket*".

Gaya's face brightened up again.

These nifty devices were amazing, but you weren't allowed to use them until you came to age because it caused a lot of distraction in school. You could wear them as a necklace, a ring, a watch, or any other personal item. Any video imaging would pop up in your normal field of vision -- these could act as a dashboard when operating machinery. I chose to pierce mine in my left ear.

I showed mine to Gaya.

"Oh wow, why did you choose to pierce yours? You look so gay with that thing on. It really fits your slender figure though, nice." Ouch.

"Thanks, well, here is my contact number" I said while I handed her a paper with my trinket id.

"Oh, yeah, thanks"

We stared at each other for a moment in silence. I didn't want our meeting to end. No one else was around at the time. She then looked to the side, facing the sun. She looked so radiant, and she was very close to me. I couldn't take it any longer. I had to do it even if she got mad. I decided to go in for a kiss.

I leaned towards her. I could hear my heart pumping faster as I was getting closer to her.

"Oh, let me put this away before I lose it" she said abruptly while she moved aside to put the paper in her bag.

My kiss attempt failed. Luckily she didn't notice me losing balance and almost planting my face on the floor.

"Well, I have to go now. I leave for East tomorrow, and I haven't packed yet. I wanted to say goodbye, so I am glad I found you."

We then hugged for a very, very short awkward moment. It wasn't even a proper hug. She only leaned her arms and head towards me, so anything below her arms was away from me, but I didn't mind. Well, I did a little bit. I didn't want her to leave.

"Bye" she said as we waved goodbye and disappeared from my sight.

"Until we meet again" was the last thing I said to her though I didn't know if I would even see her again.

Later that day I went to see Sela and Alon. We were very quiet for most of the time; just enjoying the moment that could be the last time together.

Appendix G *-- from Hadassah to Jackie*

This is how I came to be called Jackie.

My name is Hadassah, but somewhere along the road my name got changed into Jack (or Jackie), and everyone knew me by that name. I had even forgotten how it all started. The name change was no glorious thing. One day, sometime after I hit puberty Alon caught me masturbating.

"Hey Sela, I just caught Hadassah jacking off!" he yelled in pure joy "Come over!"

"Jackie!" Sela yelled. Both of them were laughing hard. I had never been so embarrassed, and they spread the news like gospel.

That was it. Ever since then 'Jackie' became my new name. Over the years everyone forgot the story -- lucky me, but the name stuck. Come to think of it, I would have much rather been called 'Cheese.'

Appendix H -- *The Priestess of Light*

The world was plagued with demons. During this era, they were the rulers of the earth, and the world trembled in fear. It was during this time when tales of the few heroes who stood against these demons, were born.

The land of the south was the home of one of the most tragic stories of these heroes.

There was a powerful demonic entity. It did not have a clear physical shape; instead, it would its body took various forms. At times it would show multiple extremities, too many to count, and at times there was more than one head that would show from the demon. This demonic entity was composed of thousands of demons that had merged to form this one powerful single manifestation that was destroying the land.

A priestess faced against the demons. They found her beautiful and full of light; a light that the demons craved. But she was not weak, and the demonic mass was hesitant in attacking her. So much light and beauty, the demons couldn't believe that there was another being that could make them feel that way -- they wanted to destroy her, drain every bit of her tasty life force until there was nothing left, but at the same time the demons wanted to protect her.

The priestess could see the conflict in the demons, and she made a deal with the entity. She would let it take her light by marrying the demon. In all the years the demons had existed for, they had never thought that they would get such a request from a mortal. The demons agreed.

By the time they were about to consummate the marriage with their thousand penises, the priestess started to proceed with her plan. She opened up her robe, and she let the demons get close. Close enough for her to trap them inside her body, the demons did not have a chance to react, they got absorbed in an instant.

Time passed by, the priestess started to be consumed by the darkness of her captives. She eventually managed to seal the demons inside her being, but the battle was too much, and dementia started to take over. Eventually, she weakened. She lost her light, and before she got overtaken by her own curse she decided to leave her people in fear that she may cause harm to those dearest to her. So she decided to wander the world.

The priestess travelled the lands until she collapsed. A group of bandits found her lying on the floor. They decided to rape her. It had been sometime since they had seen a female. She did not fight -- there was nothing much left of her conscience; a mere shell of her old powerful and beautiful self. The demons inside her urged her to get pregnant. The bandits tried to kill her after the act, but her body now belonged to her demons, she skinned the poor bastards alive.

The priestess died after giving birth. A group of nomads found the baby next to the corpse of the woman who was once invincible. Her face had a peaceful look.

Her children bore the birthmark of the demon blood -- the curse and gift of being a half--breed. The third arm of power.

Jackie (Hadassah) -- His attempt at a relationship with Haba failed miserably and in embarrassment. Jackie should have known better to not risk it all; which would then ended up in him looking desperate, and subsequently turning the girl off. Jackie then spent months upon months inside a MMO (massive multiplayer online) video game. Even there, he tried to get himself some cyber dating. That too failed. Eventually, he decided to explore the new world he was in. He got a motorcycle after getting some money from his mom. Riding his motorcycle is the one place where he finds peace, just like in his old home world. Since he doesn't work, he still lives under his mother's pension.

Haba -- age 22, four years younger than Jackie. Her youthful appearance was a reflection to her desire to take on the world with great hopes for her future. She dedicated herself to her dream of becoming the best therapist there is. She had some feelings for Jackie, but not enough to want to be with him necessarily. Besides, she was about to graduate from college and move on to another stage in her life. After Jackie went on to confess his love for her, she freaked out. She dropped all communications with him and even changed her moving plans to an earlier date.

Sonja -- age 26, she believes her best asset is her enormous large butt. She would never admit to ever farting, but the truth was different. The friction created by the two masses of fat was able to create sounds that ranged in ten octaves. She would never fart in public. This would cause her to hold all the pressure inside of her for most hours in a day. When release time came, someone could easily believe that someone was blowing on a horn.

Malak -- age 24, after she heard of the victory over Atlas; her heart beat only to the thought of seeing Jackie's face again. When she found out that she would never see him again, she was heart--broken. She believed that she would never be able to love anyone ever again. But sometime passed, and she woke up one day remembering how easy it was to order around Jackie as she pleased, and that she found to be boring. She liked to fight. She liked to have drama in her life. She wanted to do whatever she pleased. She even made out with pedophile Ham (full name: Butt Ham) one night. Eventually she started to date someone else, and then someone else after that. And she eventually ran into the man who became her husband and the father figure of her daughter.

Liora -- classmate to Jackie, same age -- she was Jackie's first major crush. No one knew for sure what it was that Jackie saw in her. Most speculated that he was infatuated with Liora's big breasts. This petite 5'4" brown eyed, curly brunette bombshell packed quite the large breasts. In fact, she was known around school for her boobs and her spunky personality. More than her magic skills, her ability to talk was quite impressive. Nobody knew where she found all the things she came up with. Some of details about her: her favorite color is green, and she loves wine -- the strong kind.

Sela -- the good old warrior; he eventually ended up settling down, with three women. It wasn't really his choice. The loss of his demonic powers led him to lose his ability to control himself during intercourse. One day, the three women came to him demanding Sela to take the responsibility. Without his powers, he could not run away from this adventure. He now goes to sleep most nights under the possession of demonic stress. Five kids later, he has lost most of his hair.

181

Umaso/Aiyoo -- he decided to keep his name as Umaso in the memory of an old friend. He leads a happy life with Gaya though he sometimes has a hard timekeeping up her demands. He has yet to gather the courage to ask her to watch her figure. She had gained twenty six pounds since they got together. After the loss of ethereal energy, her metabolism has not been able to keep up with her appetite. Speaking of which, after the defeat of the emperor; Umaso had another sparring session with Sela. This time Umaso lost; ten to two. It took both of them three months to recover. Since then, Umaso has become the victim of frequent cramps on his calves.

Shamain -- she spent a long time together with Sui Renshi, the Hero of the Sword. The warrior had spent a thousand years, and he had finally found love again after his tragic loss. One day though, Shamain got bored. She could not tolerate the smell that came off Sui Renshi's ballsack any longer. The poor soldier had never experienced such wound in his entire existence. After the break up, Shamain found herself breathing again. She travelled the world. Everywhere she went, she made new friends and countless of suitors along the way. Shamain has never been happier now that she had the freedom to be herself without any bounds. She is actively searching for ways to reach Jack. Her motives are unclear.

Cheese -- he died during the attack on colony twenty seven. It was a new residential project that orbited around Earth. He died while hiding in the closet.

Epilogue

The alarm clock reads at three twenty in the afternoon when the alarm sounds off.

A light blue colored paper lies under the clock showing a four thousand dollar repair bill on his motorcycle. Bandages lying across the floor lead to believe that our hero got himself in an accident some time ago.

Jackie tosses and turns for twenty minutes before he turns off the alarm.

He gets up after a ten hour sleep session, lazily as he massages his right shoulder. He is just too lazy to replace his old pillows despite the painful muscle stiffness he gets every time.

He skips the process of brushing his teeth. He has not stepped outside his apartment door for five days; not even to take out the garbage. He heats up some water on an electric water boiler for his instant noodles. After a moment of staring blankly at a spot for a moment, he pours the water on the noodles, and covers it.

Jackie then gets his gear ready for his journey. He turns on the computer, and puts on his headset. There's no need for a shirt or pants --or clean underwear -- on this journey. It is gaming time!

Our wounded hero has spent the past five months trying to recover from the new challenge that the world has presented him with: to keep moving on with life.

The sad part of it all is that he sucks at his games. None of the equipment in his characters is top notch.

After he received the message by Sonja; there were no new messages coming into the telecom trinket. Somehow the thing still works though the light on the ethereal core is getting dimmer. Jackie has sent some messages to his friends, just for fun and without much hope. Sometimes when he gets drunk he sends some messages that are rather sexual to all the girls in his list. He would wake up the next day terrifyed at the idea that the messages had gone through.

That is the routine of our hero, but everything is about to change once again.

One 'morning' he woke up, this time at five in the afternoon. He opened his eyes and he saw a ghastly face staring down at him.

Jackie kicked back screaming in terror as he held onto his sheets as his only shelter from this figure starting at him. The boogers on his eyes covered his visibility -- they were heavily caked on.

"Good morning"

That voice, he had not heard in years, but the familiarity made Jackie's ears crinkle. He cleared up his eyes. He could not believe the sight of the face standing there at arm's reach. Her eyes did not have their old eerie glow on them as they used to.

"Are you going to say something, or is this how you greet an old friend after so long?"

Jackie was speechless. Soon after he recognized the person in front of him; he was utterly embarassed to have her see how he had been living since they had last seen each other.

She smiled with her entire heart.

"I missed you" she said, "Hush, don't talk."

About the Author

Chung Moon graduated from the University of Tampa in 2010 with a MBA - general. After the failure of his ramen restaurant (it opened and closed within four months) and bumming around, he finally found the drive to finish this book - a project that started in 2003.

No, he is not going to write about his love for cats or anything like other authors opt to in this section. He became allergic to cats after his first one. Her name was Fairlady. She was a cute calico cat with cute pink and black colored paws. Poor thing got run over by a car one morning (April 16, 2007). The kittie considered him as mommy...

Ahem, anyways, I hope that you found this book an enjoyable read.

For more Hero of the Sword related stuff, visit http://chung-moon.blogspot.com

Thanks for reading!

www.ingramcontent.com/pod-product-compliance
Lightning Source LLC
Chambersburg PA
CBHW030253130626
46549CB00002B/514